DARREN SHAN

Birth of a Killer

THE SAGA OF LARTEN CREPSLEY: BOOK ONE

HarperCollins *Children's Books*

2o3o 0000 256 343

Darren Shan on the web is a treat wherever you come from . . .
www.darrenshan.com

First published in hardback in Great Britain by HarperCollins *Children's Books* 2010
First published in paperback in Great Britain by HarperCollins *Children's Books* 2011

HarperCollins *Children's Books* is a division of HarperCollins*Publishers* Ltd
77-85 Fulham Palace Road, Hammersmith, London W6 8JB

Visit us at www.harpercollins.co.uk

Text copyright © Darren Shan 2010

ISBN 978–0–00–731587–1

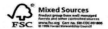

Birth of a Killer

THE SAGA OF LARTEN CREPSLEY: BOOK ONE

PART ONE

"Are cobwebs a treat where you come from?"

CHAPTER ONE

When Larten Crepsley awoke and yawned one grey Tuesday morning, he had no idea that by midday he would have become a killer.

He lay on his bed of sacks packed with straw, staring at specks of dust drifting through the air. The house where he lived was cramped and dark, and the room where he slept never caught the sun except at dawn. He often woke a few minutes earlier than necessary, before his mother roared for the family to get up. It was his only quiet time of the day, his one chance to lie back idly and grin lazily at the world.

There were six children in the room, five of them snoring and shifting in their sleep. Larten came from a crop of eight, but two had died young and his eldest sister left a year ago to marry. Although she was only fourteen, Larten suspected their parents were glad to be rid of her — she had never been an especially hard worker and brought home little money.

"Up!" Larten's mother roared from the room next to theirs, and pounded the thin wall a couple of times.

The children groaned and crawled out of bed. They bumped into one another as they tried to find their way to the bedpan, the older siblings cuffing their younger brothers and sisters. Larten lay where he was, smiling smugly. He had already done his business while everyone else was asleep.

Vur Horston shared the room with the five Crepsley children. Vur was a cousin of theirs. His parents had died when he was three years old, his father in an accident at work, his mother of some disease. Larten's mother had been keeping a close watch on the sickly widow and moved in quickly to take the baby. An extra pair of hands was always useful. The boy would be a burden for a few years, but children that age didn't eat much, and assuming Vur survived, he could be put to work young and earn his foster parents a nice little income.

Larten felt closer to Vur than to any of his real siblings. Larten had been in the kitchen when his mother brought the silent, solemn boy home. After giving Vur some bread soaked in milk — a rare treat — she'd stuck him by Larten's side and told her son to look after the waif and keep him out of her way.

Larten had eyed the newcomer suspiciously,

jealous of the gift his mother had given the stranger. In return, Vur had stared at Larten innocently, then tore the bread down the middle and offered his cousin the bigger half. They had been best friends ever since.

"Up!" Larten's mother roared again, slamming the wall just once this time. The children blinked the last traces of sleep from their eyes and quickly threw on their clothes. She would come crashing in on them soon, and if they weren't dressed and ready to go, her fists would fly.

"Vur," Larten murmured, nudging his cousin in the ribs.

"I'm awake," Vur replied, turning to show Larten his smile.

"Don't you need to go?" Larten asked.

"I'm bursting," Vur giggled.

"Hurry up!" Larten shouted at one of his younger sisters, who was squatting over the bedpan as if she owned it.

"Go in the bed if you're that desperate," she jeered.

"You might as well," Larten said to Vur. It wasn't uncommon for them to wet the bed — the great thing about straw was that it dried swiftly.

"No," Vur said, gritting his teeth. "I can wait."

Larten's clothes were on the floor next to the bed. He pulled them on, not removing the thin vest which he slept in. Larten's mother was an orderly woman. She did the family laundry every second Sunday. All the children had to wait in their beds, naked beneath the covers, until their clothes were returned. Then they would wear them without changing for the next fortnight.

Larten's sister finished on the bedpan. Before his youngest brother could claim it, Larten darted across the room, snatched it and passed it to Vur, careful not to spill the contents.

"My hero," Vur laughed, loosely aiming with one hand while he rubbed yellow crust from his eyes with the other.

Although Vur was Larten's age, he was much smaller — a thin, weak, mild-mannered boy. He seldom fought for anything, happy to go without if he was challenged. Larten often stood up for his cousin, even though Vur never asked for help.

"What's keeping you?" Larten's mother screeched, sticking her head in and glaring at the children.

"Coming!" they roared, and those nearest her ducked through the doorway even if they weren't finished dressing.

"Vur!" she yelled.

"Just a second!" he panted, straining to finish.

Larten's mother squinted at the boy, deciding

whether or not to punish him. In the end she just sniffed and withdrew. Larten sighed happily. He didn't mind when she hit him — he could take a fierce whipping — but he hated it when she hurt Vur. Larten's father almost never struck the frail orphan, but his wife whacked him as much as the others. They were all equal in her eyes.

When Vur was finished with the bedpan, Larten tossed his clothes at him and hurried down the stairs to the crowded kitchen where his brothers and sisters were already making short work of breakfast.

There was never much to eat, and those who grabbed first got the most. Their father, who'd shuffled off to work three hours earlier, had generously left some strips of pig's ears for them — he always shared what he could with his family. The older children seized upon the gristly treats with excitement. By the time Larten and Vur arrived, the strips were gone and they had to make do with stale bread and watery porridge.

Larten tore bread from the fingers of his eldest brother — they were slippery from the grease of a pig's ear — and passed it to Vur, laughing as he bobbed out of the way of his brother's swinging fist. Taking a couple of small, chipped bowls, he dipped them into the pot of porridge, filled them to the top and hurried to where Vur was waiting by the back door. He licked drips from the sides as he crossed the room, eager not to waste any.

They ate in silence, chewing the crust of the dry bread as if it was meat, using the rest to soak up the watery porridge. Larten was quicker than Vur and managed to refill his bowl before the pot was scraped bare. He ate half and saved the rest for his cousin.

It was cold and raining outside, but the kitchen was cosy. His mother hadn't lit the fire – she'd do that in the evening, when she returned from work – but the tiny room was always warm, especially with so many bodies crammed into it.

"Move on!" Larten's mother yelled, coming down the stairs. She belted those closest to her and waved a hand threateningly at the others. "Do you think I've nothing better to do than stand here watching you eat all day? Out!"

Still chewing and gulping, the children filed out into the yard, leaving their mother to mop up after them, before setting off for the first of the four inns where she cleaned.

There were two barrels of water in the yard, one for drinking, the other for washing. The Crepsley children rarely bothered with the latter barrel, but Vur went to it every morning to scrub the dirt from his face and neck. Larten had tried talking him out of his peculiar habit – the boy would shiver for half an hour on a bone-chilling morning like this – but Vur would only smile, nod and do it again the next day.

Larten drank thirstily, dipping his face into the barrel, ignoring the drops of rain that struck the back of his head. When he pulled away he left faint orange clouds in the water. His hair, like Vur's, was stained a deep orange shade. The dye was caked into his scalp, and although he could never wash it out, clots came off sometimes when he dunked his head.

He watched the clouds of dye swirling around. They were pretty. He put a finger in and splashed it about, to see what other patterns he could create. He considered calling Vur over, but the clouds were already disappearing and in a few more seconds there would be nothing for his cousin to see.

"Out of it," one of his brothers grunted, shoving Larten aside.

Larten yelled a curse and kicked out, but only hit the barrel. His brother pushed Larten again. Anger flared in the younger boy's eyes and he stepped forward for a fight. But Vur had spotted the danger and acted quickly to avert it. He didn't like it when Larten got into fights, even when he won, as he often did.

"If we don't leave now, we're going to be late," Vur warned.

"We've loads of time," Larten scowled.

"No," Vur said. "We'll be getting our heads daubed today. If we're not early, Traz will beat us."

"We got them daubed a few days ago," Larten argued.

"Trust me," Vur said. "Traz will do it again today."

Larten growled, but turned away from the barrel and sloped across to where Vur was using a scrap of cloth to pat his neck dry. There was no fixed schedule for the daubing days. Traz seemed to hand them out at random. But Vur had a knack of being able to predict when one was due. He wouldn't tell Larten how he knew, but eight times out of ten he got it right.

"Ready?" Larten asked, as if he was the one itching to leave.

"Aye," Vur said.

"Then let's go," Larten sniffed, and the two boys, neither yet a teen, headed off to work.

CHAPTER TWO

Larten and Vur wound their way through the narrow, filthy streets to the factory. Though it was early, the city was already bustling with life. In these dark autumn months you had to make the most of the sunlight.

Traders had set up stalls in the gloom before dawn and were busy haggling and selling fruit, vegetables, meat, fish, shoes, clothes, rope, pots, pans and more. Larten and Vur occasionally went to one of the big Sunday markets, where animals were traded and stalls boasted exotic wares from countries that the boys had never heard of. The pair would spend their time ogling the worldly traders and their goods, dreaming of travel and adventure. Those markets were a place of magic and mystery.

These small street stalls, on the other hand, were a nuisance. It took time to detour around the crowds, and some of the traders cuffed the boys if they drew too close — they were always wary of thieves, and one dirty street urchin looked much the same as any other. Certain traders lashed out at any child who came within striking distance.

"I want to be a trader when I grow up," Vur said, smiling as they passed a fish stall, ignoring the putrid stench.

"Aye," Larten said. "We can hunt elephants and sell their tusks."

"No," Vur shivered. "I'd be afraid they'd eat me."

"Then I'll collect the tusks and you can sell them," Larten decided.

They'd heard many tales of elephants, but had never even seen a picture of one. From the wild stories, they believed the mighty creatures were bigger than five houses, with twenty tusks, ten on either side of their trunk.

The two boys often discussed their plans for the future. The nineteenth century had dawned a few years earlier and the world was a place of mystery and intrigue, opening up to travellers more than it ever had before. Vur wanted to visit the great cities, climb the pyramids, sail across an ocean. Larten wanted to hunt tigers, elephants and whales. He knew that was unlikely, that both boys would probably remain at the factory, marry in their teens, have children of their

own and never venture beyond the outskirts of the
city where they'd been born. But he could dream. As
poor as they were, even he and Vur had the right to do
that.

They arrived fifteen minutes early for work, but
Traz was already outside the door, buckets of dye
lined up, a brush in his hand and a wicked glint in his
eyes.

Traz was their foreman. He had been at the
factory for a long time, part of the staff even when
Larten's father had worked there as a boy. He was a
cruel master, but he produced excellent results and
kept costs down, so the owners tolerated his
brutality.

Traz's eyes narrowed as the boys approached, their
heads lowered and knees trembling. Part of the fun for
him on daubing days was catching the children by
surprise. He loved it when they turned up on time,
only to find themselves at the back of a line. By the
time he'd processed those ahead of them, the children
at the rear would be late and Traz could legitimately
beat them.

Traz disliked the Horston boy intensely. The pale
weakling was too smart for his own good. He did a fine
job of hiding his intelligence, but he gave himself away
at times like this. Only the shrewder children were

able to second-guess Traz. These two almost always turned up early on daubing days, and he was certain that the Crepsley brat wasn't the brains of the outfit.

"You're early!" Traz barked when the boys stopped before him, as if being early was a crime.

"Our mother had to leave earlier than usual today," Larten muttered. "She threw us out, so we came here."

Traz glowered at them, but decided not to press the matter. Others were already arriving and he didn't want to waste too much time on the daubings — he would take the blame if production dipped.

"Bend over," he grunted and grabbed the back of Larten's neck. Thrusting the boy down, he reached into the bucket of orange dye with his brush, swished it from side to side, then ran the coarse bristles over the top of Larten's scalp. The dye stung, and a few drops trickled into Larten's eyes, even though he kept them squeezed shut.

Traz painted Larten's head a second time, then a third, before releasing him. As Larten staggered away, coughing and wiping his eyes, Traz forced Vur down over the bucket. He was even rougher with Vur and daubed his scalp five times. Vur was crying when the foreman finally let him go, but he said nothing, only stumbled along after his cousin.

Traz daubed the head of every child in the factory. Each had a specific colour, depending on their job. The lucky few who worked on the looms were blue. Cleaners were yellow. Cocooners were orange. He liked being able to tell with a single look where a child was meant to be. That way, if he saw an orange-haired boy lurking by a loom, he knew straightaway that the child was shirking.

Larten and Vur had been assigned to the cocooning team when they started at the factory at the age of eight. Their heads had been orange ever since. In fact Larten couldn't remember what colour his hair had been before that.

Larten's father had been a muscular child and had worked on a team carting heavy loads around. His head had been dyed white, and although he'd left the factory before Larten was born, his locks had kept their unnatural colour, so Larten had resigned himself to a life of orange hair. Nobody knew what sort of poisons Traz included in his dyes, but they seeped into a person's pores and remained there for life. Larten wouldn't be surprised if the dye had even turned his brain a dark orange colour.

Once past Traz, the boys made their way to the room of cocoons to begin their shift. They worked in the factory for twelve hours a day, six days a week, and eight hours on most Sundays, with no more than a handful of holidays every year. It was a hard life, yet there were others worse off than Larten and Vur. Some of the children were slaves, bought by Traz from poor or greedy parents. The slaves worked constantly, except for when they slept. They were supposed to be set free once they came of age, but most died long before that. Even if they lived long enough to earn their freedom, they were usually ruined by that time, good for nothing except stealing or begging.

The factory primarily produced carpets, but it also manufactured silk clothes for patrons with more money than Larten or Vur could dream of ever possessing. Silk came from worms, and the boys were part of the team responsible for loosening the strands of the worms' cocoons.

Silk worms hatched from the eggs of carefully bred moths, and were fed on chopped mulberry leaves to fatten them up. They were kept in a warm room, countless thousands stacked on wooden trays from floor to ceiling, munching away. Larten had been in the room a few times and the sound was like the rain falling on the roof of their house during a storm.

When they had eaten enough, the silk worms spun

a cocoon around themselves. It took three or four days. After that they were stored in an even warmer room for eight or nine days, then baked in an oven to kill the worm, but preserve the cocoon.

That was when Larten, Vur and their team went into action. When the cocoons were delivered, they sorted through them, dividing them into piles on the basis of size, colour and quality. Then they dipped the cocoons into vats of hot water to loosen the threads. Once they'd done that, they passed the cocoons to another team, whose members unwound the threads onto spools, which were finally given to the weavers at the looms.

Although Larten couldn't remember what colour his hair had been when he first came to the factory, he would never forget the first time he dunked his hands in a vat of near-boiling water. Traz watched, smiling, as the boy worked up the courage to stick in his fingers. The foreman laughed when Larten touched the hot water and jerked away with a yelp. Then he grabbed the boy's hands by the wrists and jammed them in. He held them under, chuckling sadistically while Larten cried and his flesh reddened.

Larten studied his fingers. They were callused, stained and cut in many places. He didn't mind the calluses and stains, but the cuts worried him. Silk worms were disgusting, filthy creatures. Larten had seen many of his team lose a finger or a hand when a dirt-encrusted cut became infected. Some had even died of blood-poisoning.

There was nothing worse than the stench of gangrene. Sometimes a child tried to hide an infected wound in the vain hope that it would miraculously cure itself. But the smell always gave them away, and Traz would gleefully cut out the rot with a heated knife, or hack off the diseased limb with an axe.

Larten lived in fear of infection. He hoped he would have the courage, if the day ever came, to cut himself before Traz could, and cleanse the wound with a firing brand. But he knew it would be a difficult thing to do, and he was afraid he'd try to hide it as so many others had before him.

"I see some green," Vur murmured, looking closely at Larten's left hand. Larten's heart beat faster and his head darted forward. Then he caught Vur's smile.

"Cur!" he growled, playfully punching his cousin.

"They're fine," Vur laughed. "The sweetest pair of hands in the factory. Now let's stop wasting time. There are cocoons to boil."

Sighing, Larten reached into his bucket. He took out a few cocoons, steadied himself, then drove his hands deep into the heart of the bubbling vat. The pain was fierce to begin with, but after a few seconds his toughened flesh adjusted and he worked without complaint for the rest of the morning.

CHAPTER THREE

The hours passed slowly and quietly. Dunking cocoons wasn't a demanding job and boredom quickly set in. Larten would have loved to chat with Vur and the others on his team. But Traz prowled the factory relentlessly, and although he was a large man, he could move as lithely as a cat. If the foreman caught you talking, he would whip you until he drew blood. There was a rumour that he'd once cut out a girl's tongue and kept it in his wallet. So all of them went about their business in silence, only talking if it was work-related.

The fires beneath the vats were kept burning around the clock – slaves worked throughout the night – and the room was forever smoke-filled. It wasn't long before the children were coughing and spitting, rubbing grit from their eyes. Larten could never get the taste of smoke out of his mouth. Even in dreams his tongue was heavy with soot.

His clothes stank too, as did Vur's. Some nights, when Larten's mother was in a foul mood, she would scream at the boys and force them to undress. She'd toss their clothes into the yard and they'd have to go to bed early to hide their naked bodies from Larten's jeering brothers and sisters.

Larten's father hadn't wanted to send the boys to the factory. He hated the place as much as they did, even though he'd escaped and now laboured elsewhere. He had managed to find work in other areas for the older children, but jobs were scarce when it came time for Larten and Vur to earn a living. The silk factory had recently won a lucrative contract and Traz was offering halfway decent wages. There was nowhere else for the unlucky pair to go.

Larten had to keep the fire beneath his vat at a constant heat. As soon as he felt the temperature of the water dropping, he fed the flames with an armful of logs from a mound at the back of the room.

Across from him, Vur finished dunking another batch of cocoons, then set off at a jog for the pit out back. Traz reluctantly accepted the need for toilet breaks, but if he caught you walking instead of running, you were guaranteed a whipping.

Larten grinned. Vur had a weak bladder and most days he had to go to the pit three times to Larten's once. Vur tried drinking less, but it made no difference. Traz had beaten him in the early days, when he thought the boy was making excuses. But eventually he realised that Vur's complaint was genuine, and though he still cuffed Vur occasionally, he let the wretch go as often as he needed to.

Vur looked worried when he returned this time.

"What's wrong?" Larten whispered.

"One of the owners was with Traz," Vur panted. "They were on their way to inspect the room of baby worms."

Word spread and everyone upped the tempo. It was bad news whenever one of the owners came to visit. Traz got nervous in the presence of his employers. He would meekly lead his boss around, a false smile plastered in place, sweating like a pig. As soon as the visitor departed, Traz would take a few swigs from a bottle of rum that he kept in his office, then storm furiously through the factory, finding fault wherever he looked.

They were hard days when Traz was on the warpath. No matter what you did, he could turn on you. Even the most skilful workers on the looms – normally the best treated in the factory – had suffered lashings at times like this.

Larten prayed while he worked, begging a variety

of gods to keep Traz away from their vats. Though Larten wasn't religious, he figured there was no harm in covering all the angles when trouble was in the air.

They heard a roar and every child lowered their head and dunked cocoons as fast as they could. The problem was, they had to leave them in the water until the cocoons had softened properly. If Traz found hard cocoons in their baskets it would be far worse than if he thought they were going slow.

Traz entered like a bear, growling and glaring, hoping someone would glance up at him. But all the children stared fixedly into their vats. He was pleased to see that most of them were trembling. That sapped some of the fire from his rage, but he needed to hand out three or four more beatings before he'd really start to calm down.

A girl lost her grip on a couple of cocoons as Traz was passing and they bobbed to the surface. He was on her like a hawk. "Keep them down!" he bellowed, swatting the back of her head. She winced and drove the cocoons to the base of the vat, soaking the sleeves of her dress.

"Sorry, sir," the girl gasped.

Traz grabbed her hair – she was new to the team and had made the mistake of not cutting it short – and jerked her face up to his. "If you ever do that again," he snarled, "I'll bite off your nose."

It would have been funny if anyone else had made such a ludicrous threat. But Traz had bitten off more than one nose in his time — a good number of ears too — and they all knew that he meant it. Nobody snickered.

Traz released the girl. He wasn't interested in newcomers. He knew the younger children were terrified of him and probably dreamt about him when they went to bed every night. They were too easy to scare. He wanted to work on some of the more experienced hands, remind a few of the older lot of his power, make sure they didn't start taking him for granted.

He cast his gaze around. There was a tall boy in one corner, a lazy piece of work. Traz started to move in on him, but then he caught sight of Vur Horston and changed direction.

Traz slowly strolled past Vur, giving him the impression that he'd escaped the foreman's wrath. But when he was about four strides past he stopped, turned and stepped up behind the boy.

Vur knew he was in trouble, but he worked on, not giving any sign that he was aware of Traz's presence. Larten could see that his cousin was in for a beating, and although he risked drawing attention to himself, he raised his head slightly to watch. He felt sick and hateful, but there was nothing he could do.

For a while Traz didn't say anything, just studied Vur as he dunked cocoons and held them beneath the surface of the water. Then he stuck a thick, dirty finger into the vat and held it there for a couple of seconds.

"Lukewarm," he said, withdrawing the finger and sucking it dry.

Vur gulped, but didn't move. He wanted to throw more sticks on the fire – even though the heat was fine – but he had to keep the cocoons down. If he released them early, he'd be in an even worse situation than he was now.

Behind Vur's back, Traz scowled. He'd hoped the boy would panic, release the cocoons and give the foreman an excuse to batter him.

"You're a vile, useless piece of work," Traz said. He tried to think of something more cutting, then recalled someone telling him that the boy was an orphan. "An insult to the memory of your mother," Traz added, and was delighted to note the boy's back stiffen with surprise and anger.

"You didn't know that I knew your mother, did you?" Traz said slyly, walking around the vat, cracking his knuckles, warming to the game.

"No, sir," Vur croaked.

"She didn't work here, did she?"

"No."

"So where do you think I knew her from?"

Vur shook his head. Across from him, Larten guessed what the foreman was up to, but there was no way he could warn Vur. He just hoped that Vur was reading Traz's intentions too. Usually Vur was a better judge of people than Larten was, but fear had a way of shaking up a person's thoughts.

"Well?" Traz purred.

"I don't know, sir."

"Inns," Traz declared grandly. "I knew her from inns."

Vur's head rose and he frowned. Larten groaned — his cousin had swallowed the bait. This was going to be bad.

"Beg pardon, sir, but you're mistaken. My mother didn't work in an inn."

"She did," Traz sniffed.

"No, sir," Vur said. "She was a seamstress."

"By day," Traz jeered. "But she earned a bit extra by night." He gave Vur a few seconds to dwell on that. "Worked in a lot of inns. I met with her many times."

Vur was too young to have kissed a girl, but there were few true innocents in the world at that time. He knew what the foreman was implying. His cheeks flushed. The worst thing was, he couldn't say for sure that it was a lie. He was almost certain that Traz was toying with him, but Vur had few memories of his parents, so he couldn't dismiss the insult as an outrageous piece of slander.

"She wasn't a pretty thing," Traz continued, relishing the twisted look on Vur's face. "But she was pretty good at her job. Aye?"

Vur started to tremble, but not with fear. He had always been able to control his temper — much better than Larten could — but he'd never been subjected to an insult of this nature before.

Traz whispered something in Vur's ear. The boy's face went white and a lone cocoon bobbed up inside the vat.

"Keep the bloody things down!" Traz roared, punching Vur hard in the left side of his head. Vur was slugged sideways and lost his grip on the cocoons. They all shot to the top. "Idiot!" Traz yelled and followed it up with cruder curses, each accompanied by a blow to Vur's head.

Vur tried to push the cocoons down again, but was knocked away from the vat by the bullying foreman, then to the ground. As he hit the floor, Traz kicked the boy in the stomach. Vur cried out with pain, then threw up over Traz's boot.

The foreman's fury doubled. Cursing the boy with his vilest insults, he grabbed cocoons from the vat and lobbed them at Vur's face. Vur retreated like a crab, trying to avoid the soggy missiles. Larten and the others watched with their jaws open. They had never seen Traz as mad as this. Nobody was bothering with work any longer. All eyes were on the furious bully and his defenceless victim.

When the vat ran out, Traz plucked cocoons from the vat next to it. He had never before manhandled the valuable balls of silken thread, but something inside him had snapped. It wasn't anything Vur had said or done. This had been building within the hate-filled foreman for a long time, and Vur was simply in the wrong place at the worst possible moment.

Traz stamped after the fleeing Vur, pelting him with cocoons, calling the boy and his mother all sorts of disgusting names. Larten saw Vur getting close to the door and prayed his cousin wouldn't make it. He had a vision of Traz slamming the door shut on Vur, over and over, smashing the bony boy to pieces. It would be better if Vur collapsed in the middle of the floor. All Traz could hit him with then would be his fists, feet and cocoons.

As if responding to Larten's silent prayer, Vur stopped crawling and held his ground ahead of the advancing foreman. But Vur hadn't stopped to take a beating. Something had switched inside him, just as it had inside the vicious Traz. He knew it was lunacy, but he couldn't stop himself. Maybe it was a reaction to one of the insults aimed at his dead mother. Maybe a bone had shattered in his ribs and the pain drove him momentarily insane. Or maybe life had been leading him to this point since he first stepped into the factory, and it was simply his destiny to one day hit back at a world that treated helpless children so repulsively.

Vur snatched a cocoon from the floor, hurled it at Traz and screamed, "Leave me alone, you…" He paused as the cocoon struck Traz between his eyes, then smiled and finished with an insult every bit as crude as any the foreman had used.

Traz came to a stunned halt. The cocoon had only left a wet, slimy mark behind, and he'd been called far worse in his time by drunkards, scoundrels and women of ill repute. But no child had ever spoken that way to him. And he had never been struck in front of a crowd of gawping children.

Traz was a beastly man and always had been. But in that second he slipped beyond the boundaries of mere brutality. He had beaten children senseless in the past. He had chewed off noses and ears, and the story about cutting out a girl's tongue was true. Children had died under his watch from festering wounds and starvation, and he had laughed at their agonies. But he had never set out to openly murder one of his crew.

As the cocoon dripped on the floor and the echoes of Vur's curse died away, Traz lost control of himself. It was abrupt and awful, and before anyone knew it was coming, he had already launched himself at the boy.

Traz scooped Vur up from the floor with one huge paw. Vur cursed him again and hit him with a fist instead of a soft cocoon. But Traz was in no mood to play. Instead of beating the boy, he swept Vur over to the nearest vat and shoved a cringing girl out of his way. Before Vur could protest, Traz upended him and thrust him underwater, pushing him all the way to the bottom and holding his head there with one thick, hairy, powerful hand.

Vur kicked out wildly. One of his feet struck Traz's chin. The foreman grunted and slipped. Vur bobbed to the surface like a cocoon. But then Traz regained his balance and pushed Vur down again, using his free arm to bend back the boy's legs. Ignoring the heat of the water, he held Vur in place, fingers squeezed tight into the flesh of the boy's skull.

"Let him go!" Larten shouted, surprising even himself.

Traz's eyes flared and he bared his teeth. "Stay out of this!"

"Stop it!" Larten cried. "You'll kill him!"

"Aye," Traz chuckled. "That's what I'm aiming to do."

Larten had lived in fear of the foreman since the age of eight, but there was no time for terror on that cold, grey Tuesday. Vur was drowning. Larten had to act swiftly or it would be too late.

Abandoning the safety of his vat, Larten raced towards the laughing Traz and threw himself at the monstrous man. The floor was wet and he hoped Traz would lose his footing when he was tackled. If he could get Vur out of the vat, they'd flee like rats and never come back. His father wouldn't care, not when Larten told him what had happened. There were limits to what even the likes of Traz could get away with.

But Traz had clocked the Crepsley boy's every move. He anticipated the leap and adjusted his stance. When Larten threw himself forward, Traz simply let go of Vur's legs – not thrashing now – and slammed a fist down on Larten's skull.

Larten felt as if his head had been caved in. For a few seconds he came close to blacking out. He would have fainted any other time, but he knew Vur needed him. He couldn't afford to fall unconscious. So, drawing strength from deep within himself, he shook his head and lurched to his knees.

Traz was surprised. He thought he'd killed the boy, or at least hit him so hard that he'd slump around simple-minded for the rest of his days. Even in the midst of his murderous fit he found himself respecting the way Larten hauled himself up, first to his knees, then to his feet. His legs were swaying like a drunk's, but Traz admired the boy for rising to make a challenge.

The worst of the foreman's rage ebbed away and he grunted. "Stay down, you fool."

Larten moaned in reply and staggered forward. This time he didn't try to hit the huge man. He was only focused on Vur's legs. They were as still as a crushed dog's and Larten knew he had mere seconds in which to fish out his cousin — if it wasn't already too late.

Traz squinted at the advancing child. When he realised Larten was only worried about the drowning boy, Traz looked down and hissed. Vur Horston was no longer moving and no bubbles of air were trickling from his mouth.

Traz felt no guilt, merely unease. Though he doubted his employers would care too much if word of this incident reached them, there was always the possibility that they might decide he had gone too far. Releasing Vur's legs, he stepped away from the vat and wrung water from the sleeves of his jacket, thinking hard.

Not being a man of the world like Traz, Larten thought there was still hope. He gurgled happily when Traz moved aside, then gripped Vur's legs and dragged him out of the vat. His cousin was heavier than normal, his clothes soaked, and Larten was still dizzy from the blow to his head. But it only took him a couple of seconds to pull Vur clear and lay him on the floor.

"Vur!" Larten called, sprawling beside his motionless cousin. When there was no answer, he turned Vur's head sideways and prised his lips apart to let water out. "Vur!" He slapped the silent boy's back. "Are you all right? Can you hear me? Did he—"

"Silence!" Traz barked. When Larten glanced up, blinking back tears, the foreman added coldly, "There's nothing you can do for him. The gutter rat's dead. All that's left for him now is the grave."

CHAPTER FOUR

As the world seemed to spin wildly around the dazed, sickened Larten, Traz faced the rest of the cocooners. He was only worried about protecting his job. He didn't care a shred for the bedraggled remains of the murdered Vur Horston.

"Listen up!" Traz roared, glaring at one and all. "The savage little rat attacked me. Everybody saw it. I was defending myself and it'll go bad with anyone who says different."

Traz cast his gaze around, challenging the children to disagree with him. They all dropped their heads and Traz puffed up proudly. He had nothing to fear. None of these cowards would speak out against him.

"I'm going to hang his body off a hook out back," Traz boasted. "I want you to study it long and hard before you go home. This is what happens to vicious fools who attack their foremen. We won't be having any revolutions in *this* factory!"

Already, in his mind, he was exaggerating the boy's act of defiance. He would tell the owners that several of the brats attacked him. Claim it was an organised revolt, that the Horston boy was its leader. Fake regret and say that he had to kill Vur for the good of the factory. Let them believe there were others who were plotting against them. If they believed there was a threat to their profits, they'd give Traz a medal for working so hard to suppress it.

Men of wealth were easy to appease. If you kept money flowing into their pockets, they backed every move you made. They wouldn't care that he'd killed an orphan, not as long as he could put a price on the cur's head.

On the floor, Larten was staring at Vur with horror. The dead boy's right eye was closed, but his left was open a fraction, as if he was winking. Larten wished Vur *was* playing a joke. He wouldn't mind if his cousin sat up and laughed at him for falling for the trick. Larten would cry with joy if that happened.

But Vur wasn't acting. Larten had seen death many times — an older sister, children in the factory, corpses in the street waiting to be collected. There was no mistaking the chilling stillness of the dead.

"Out of my way," Traz sneered, pushing Larten aside.

Larten hadn't been focusing on Traz's speech. He didn't know what the foreman intended to do with Vur. In his bewildered state, he thought Traz was trying to help.

"It's no good," Larten whispered. "You can't help him. He's dead."

Traz cocked an eyebrow at Larten and laughed. "*Help him?* Didn't you hear me? I'm going to hang him from a hook and teach you all a lesson."

Larten gawped at the burly foreman.

"Go home to your father," Traz huffed. "Tell him he's lucky I let *you* live. I could have killed you too for attacking me. But because I'm a merciful man, I'm letting you go."

Larten didn't move. He had been crying, but the tears dried up now and a cold fire ignited at the back of his eyes.

"Go on," Traz said, picking up Vur and slinging him over a shoulder as if he was a sack of cocoons. "You can have the afternoon off. But be back here first thing tomorrow. And tell your father he can pick this one up on Friday — I want to hang him for a few days like a pheasant."

As Traz turned away, Larten calmly picked something off the floor. He would never remember what he'd grabbed. The area was littered with every sort of cast-off — nails, old spools, broken knives and more. All he knew was that it was sharp and cool, and it fitted perfectly into his small, trembling hand.

"Traz," Larten said with surprising softness. If he'd screamed, maybe the foreman would have sensed danger and jerked aside. As it was, Traz simply paused and looked back, half smiling the way he would if an old friend hailed him in a park on a Sunday.

Larten stepped forward and drove his hand up. The boy's eyes were flat, as devoid of expression as Vur's, but his mouth was twisted into a dark, leering grin, as something vile and inhuman inside him rejoiced at being set free.

When Larten lowered his hand, whatever he'd picked up was no longer in his palm. The object was now buried deep in Traz's throat.

Traz stared at Larten through a pair of wide, bulging eyes. He didn't drop Vur. Indeed, his grip on the boy tightened. With his free hand he tried to pull out the object that was stuck in his windpipe. But there was no strength in his fingers and the flesh around his neck was slippery with blood. His arm fell by his side. He opened his mouth and tried to say something, but only blood gurgled out.

Still staring at Larten, Traz fell to his knees, swayed

for a moment, then slumped. He lost hold of Vur and the boy's body rolled away from him.

The silence in the room was more frightening than any bellow of Traz's had ever been. The children were transfixed. Vur's death had been unexpected, but it hardly counted as a cataclysmic event in this factory of misery. But the slaying of Traz had shaken their world to its core. Nothing could be the same after this.

Larten licked his lips and began to lean forward. The hateful thing inside him wanted to retrieve the object from Traz's throat and use it to stab out the dead foreman's eyes. But as his fingers stretched out before him, he shuddered and blinked, then took a step backwards, shocked by what he had done and had been planning to do.

Feeling sick and bewildered, Larten took a couple more steps away. As he was backing up, his gaze flickered from Traz to Vur, and realisation of what he'd done struck him like a lightning bolt. He had killed a man. And not just any man, but Traz, the darling of the owners. Nobody in the neighbourhood liked Traz, but he had been respected. Larten would have to answer for the foreman's death, and he knew what form that answer would take — a carefully knotted hangman's noose.

Larten didn't try to appeal to the other children, to

ask them for help or to lie on his behalf. They owed him nothing. If they stood by his side or tried to hide his identity, they would suffer too.

Turning wildly, fighting against a wave of bile, Larten searched desperately for the door — he had become disoriented and didn't know where it was. As soon as he sighted it, he ran for his life.

As if the children had been waiting for this signal, one of them raised a finger, pointed at the fleeing boy and screeched, *"Murderer!"*

Within seconds they were all screaming Larten's name, pointing, howling like banshees. But they did nothing except scream. No one tried to follow him. There was no need. Others would take care of that. A full, fearsome mob of righteous executioners would soon be hot on Larten's trail, each member of the pack eager to be the first to string up the cold-blooded, orange-haired killer.

CHAPTER FIVE

Larten ran without any real sense of direction. He hadn't explored much of the city beyond his own neighbourhood, but he knew every last inch of the area around the factory, all the alleys, roads, ruins and hiding places. If he had been thinking straight, he could have slipped away quickly and cleanly, or found a spot where he could hide until night.

But Larten was in a panic. His best friend had been murdered in front of him and he'd killed a man in response. His heart was pounding and he fell often, scraping his legs and hands. His head was a bedlam of noise and terror, his only clear thought, *"Run!"*

If a mob had formed swiftly, they would have found Larten flailing around the streets outside the factory, losing his way and backtracking, an easy target. But the adults who answered the calls of the children were thunderstruck. They pressed the witnesses for detailed descriptions of Traz's last moments. If anyone had thought to give chase, others would have immediately joined them. But in the chaos, everyone assumed that a group was already in pursuit of the boy, so precious minutes passed without anybody making a move.

Outside, Larten had turned down a dead-end alley. He was looking behind him for pursuers, so he ran into a wall and fell with a cry. As he picked himself up and rubbed his head, he spotted a girl no more than four or five, sitting on a step and studying him.

"What are you doing?" she asked.

Larten shook his head.

"You're hurt," the girl said.

Larten didn't know what she was talking about. When she pointed at his head, he rubbed it again, looked at his fingers and saw that he was bleeding. Now that he was aware of his wound, pain kicked in and he grimaced.

"My mummy can fix you," the girl said. "She fixes me when I get hurt."

"That's all right," Larten croaked. "I'll be fine."

"She gives me a cup of tea with sugar," the girl said. "*Sugar*," she repeated boastfully. "Have you ever had sugar?"

"No," Larten said.

"It's lovely," she whispered.

Larten stared around. The worst of the panic had passed. He wasn't sure why, but he didn't feel so afraid any more. He was still a long way from normal, yet he began thinking of what he should do and where he could go. He had to get away quickly, but he'd only be able to do that if he held his nerve.

"Thank you," he said to the girl and headed back up the alley.

"For what?" the girl asked.

"Calming me down."

She giggled. "You're silly. Come back and play."

But Larten had no time to waste on play. There was only one game of any interest to him now — *beat the hangman*.

From the alley he took a right turn and had soon left behind the neighbourhood where he'd spent all his life. Though he wasn't sure of the surrounding area, he had a vague idea of the shape of the city and moved in an eastern direction. That was his quickest route to the outskirts. He didn't run, but walked briskly, head down, not making eye contact with anyone.

Nobody paid attention to the thin, dirty, bloodied, trembling boy. The city was full of lost, wounded strays just like him.

At the factory, someone finally asked what had become of Traz's killer. When people realised the boy had escaped without even a half-hearted challenge, they were outraged — nobody had liked Traz, but a rebellious brat like Larten Crepsley couldn't be allowed to stab a hard-working foreman to death and waltz away freely. A gang took to the streets and was soon joined by dozens of others as word of the murder spread. Life was monotonous in those parts and a chase was a major attraction. Men, women and teenagers joined the workers from the factory, brandishing knives, hooks and any other sharp implements they could find. More than one also took the time to root out a good length of rope. Mobs were never shy of volunteers when it came to the office of hangman.

By the time the mob was fully formed and storming through the streets, Larten was out of danger's immediate range. Their cries didn't reach him or alert any of the people he was passing. With no sign of a chase party, he was able to keep calm and carry on at a steady pace.

It never crossed his mind to go home. He knew that was the first place the mob would look for him, but that wasn't the reason he avoided it. If he thought his parents would try to protect him, he might have returned. If he believed people would grant him a fair hearing, maybe he wouldn't have fled. If there was any justice in the world, perhaps he'd have thrown himself at the feet of his accusers and begged for mercy.

But nobody would care about Vur Horston. Children in factories were killed all the time. As long as the owners made money, they didn't mind. But the killing of a foreman was a scandal. An example would have to be made, to stop other workers from following Larten's lead.

Larten's father was a thoughtful, caring man, and his gruff mother loved him in her own way, but life was hard and poor people had to be practical. They couldn't save him from the mob, and Larten didn't think they'd even try. He figured they would hand him over and curse him for being a fool and losing his temper.

Larten had never heard the phrase, "burning your bridges". But he would have understood it. There was no home for him in this city any more. He was all alone in the world, and marked for death.

It was evening by the time Larten cleared the city. The sky had been dark all day, and now it began to blacken with the coming of night. There was a cruel bite to the air. Larten had no coat and he shivered in his short-sleeved shirt. He was hungry and thirsty, but the cold was his main concern. He had to find shelter or he'd end up like one of the stiff, frozen street people he'd often seen.

Hunching his shoulders against the cold, Larten walked along the main road for a while, then took a dirt track. His vague plan was to find a village and lay up in a cowshed or barn. He didn't know how long a walk it would be, but he guessed it couldn't be more than a few miles.

If it hadn't started to rain heavily, Larten would have kept going. Maybe he'd have slipped along the way, twisted an ankle and perished of the wet and cold in the open. Or maybe he'd have made good time and found shelter, stolen a few eggs in the morning and set off in search of a job. He might have scraped by, worked hard, earned some money. Perhaps he'd have lived a good life, married and had children, and died at the ripe old age of forty or forty-five.

But Larten's destiny didn't lie in a ditch or any of the nearby villages. Rain soaked him, forcing him to look for immediate shelter. A tree would have been fine, but the clouds looked thundery and he'd heard tales of people who had been struck by lightning under trees. There were no caves that he knew of. That left...

Larten looked around, praying for inspiration, and through a brief break in the rain his prayers were answered. He spotted the heads of tombstones and realised he was close to a graveyard.

Larten had only been to a graveyard once before, one Sunday when he and Vur had trekked to the northern part of town where a large cemetery stood. They'd gone hoping to see ghosts, having heard tales of headless horsemen roaming the rows of graves. Of course they didn't see any – ghosts mostly came out at night – but they saw plenty of monuments to the dead.

The poor of the city were carted off to be dumped in mass graves, nothing to mark the spot where they lay. Those with money secured a grave. Wealthy people bought tombs.

Graves and tombs were of no use to Larten, but some of the truly rich invested in family crypts, small houses for the dead. If they kept the dead dry, they could keep the living dry too, at least for a night.

Larten didn't know if this small graveyard would boast any crypts. But on the off-chance he abandoned the path and splashed through sodden fields, fearfully edging his way towards the home of the (hopefully) sleeping dead.

CHAPTER SIX

The graveyard was larger than Larten had imagined, and while it was no match for the lavish city of the dead to the north, there were a few crypts jutting out of the crop of crosses and tombs.

Larten scrambled across the graves, muttering prayers to every god he'd ever heard of, eyes cast low. He wanted to look every which way at once, to check for ghosts, witches, demons. But he thought that if he saw them, they would see him too. By not looking, he hoped no ghosts would notice him, so he kept his eyes on the ground. It was a foolish notion, but it gave Larten the courage to go on.

He couldn't get into the first crypt that he tried — the doors were sealed shut. There was a chain on the woven copper gates of the next. He tugged at the gates as hard as he could, and the chain gave a little, but not enough.

Larten thought he heard movement behind him.

He stood, head lowered, expecting an attack. When nothing leapt out of the growing darkness, he looked around for another crypt, then hurried towards it.

He almost didn't try this door. It was on hinges and slightly ajar, but it was carved of stone and he doubted he had the strength to move it. But rain was lashing down, exhaustion had set deep into his bones, and the next crypt was some way off. So, with no real hope, he grabbed the edge of the door and pulled.

The door slid open so smoothly that he slipped and fell. Landing with a splash in a puddle of rain and mud, he tensed and peered into the darkness. Maybe the door had opened so easily because something inside had pushed out at the same time that he'd pulled. But if a ghost was lurking within, Larten couldn't see it.

"*Are you mad?*" a voice very much like Vur's whispered inside his head. "*Don't go in there. It's a place for the dead.*"

But Larten was out of options. If he didn't find shelter here, he doubted he'd find it anywhere. As terrified as he was by the thought of spending the night in a crypt, he had a better chance in there than out here. So, with one last quick prayer, he got to his feet, wiped his hands dry on his trousers, then ducked and entered the crypt.

At first he thought it was pitch black. But he closed his eyes for a while, and when he opened them again he could see fairly well. There were glass panels in the ceiling. That seemed strange to Larten, but maybe some of the people buried here had been afraid of the dark.

He remained by the door while his eyes adjusted, then studied the crypt. There were brick walls on either side, behind which the coffins were stacked. A strange sort of ornamental fountain in the middle. No sign of any ghosts.

Growing braver, Larten moved away from the door, into the centre of the crypt. It was cool here, but warmer than outside and a lot drier. He rubbed his arms up and down, trying to generate heat. He'd have to take his clothes off later to let them dry, but he was wary of undressing too soon in case a ghost rose from one of the coffins and attacked. He didn't want to have to flee naked through the graveyard!

Larten chuckled weakly at the image. Then his stomach rumbled and he winced. He'd been hungry for a long time, but had been able to ignore it. Now his hunger kicked in hard. If only the owner had come to the factory after lunch. The children didn't get much in the middle of the day, but a few scraps of bread and some slops of watery soup would have made a big difference. Trust Traz to pick the worst possible time to get killed.

Larten chuckled again. He knew murder was wrong, and he wished he could go back and change this day, but in all honesty he wasn't sad that Traz was dead. He and Vur had often prayed for the gods to strike down their bullying foreman. He didn't think too many people would shed tears on Traz's account.

As Larten approached the fountain, he saw that it was covered in cobwebs. He scanned the strands for spiders – he'd eaten insects before when food was scarce – but they were either hiding or had moved on. Sighing, he figured he might as well try the webs since there was nothing else available. He doubted they'd fill him up – they might even make him sick – but what choice did he have?

He ran a couple of fingers through one of the webs, breaking the strands. Then he twirled his fingers around several times, adding to the webby covering. When it was thick enough to hide his flesh, he brought his fingers to his mouth, shut his eyes and peeled off the webs with his teeth.

Larten gagged on the foul-tasting webs and almost vomited, but then he gulped and forced down the disgusting, dusty strands. After a brief pause for breath, he scooped up more, working his way down from the top of the fountain. He kept looking for spiders or even a few desiccated flies, but no joy.

Then, out of the solemn, sinister silence of the crypt, as he was sucking more of the spider's silk from his sticky fingers, someone spoke from a spot high above and behind him.

"Are cobwebs a treat where you come from?"

Larten whirled, eyes locking on the wall above the door, the one place he hadn't thought to check when he'd entered the crypt. Something was attached to the bricks. It was a red-skinned beast, with a pale face and long dark hair streaked with white. Its claws were dug into the bricks and it was studying Larten with what seemed to be a wicked, bloodthirsty smile.

Larten darted for the door, certain he was too late, that the creature would drop in front of him and block his way, before falling upon him and finishing him off. But to his surprise the beast never moved and a second later Larten was in the doorway, freedom a couple of paces ahead of him.

"I would ask you to stay a while," the creature murmured, and something in its tone made Larten pause. He cast a quick glance upwards and saw that the thing had lowered its head. Only a handful of inches now separated their faces.

Larten squealed and slammed against the jamb of the doorway. But still he didn't spill out of the crypt and run away. Because the creature hadn't sounded threatening when it spoke. It had sounded strangely *lonely*.

"What are you?" Larten gasped.

"Should not the question be *who* am I?" the creature asked, then released its grip, dropped to the floor and stood. Larten saw that it was actually a man — or at least it had the body and face of one. The red he'd glimpsed was the material of the man's clothes, not his skin, which – from what Larten could see – was no different to any other person's.

"Aren't you a monster?" Larten frowned, eyeing the man suspiciously.

"I would not describe myself as one," the man chuckled, "although there are many who would."

To Larten's surprise, the man extended a hand. Larten's heart was pounding, but it would be rude to refuse this gesture of friendship. Sticking out a trembling hand of his own, he accepted the man's offer of a handshake. The man's grip was loose, but Larten sensed immense strength in the fingers.

"My name is Seba Nile," the man said, "and this is my home for the night. You are more than welcome to share it with me if you wish."

"Thank you," Larten said weakly, feeling like he was in a dream. "My name's Larten Crepsley."

"I bid you welcome, Larten," Seba said warmly, and without releasing the boy's hand, he led him back into the shadows of the crypt.

CHAPTER SEVEN

Seba Nile sat on the floor, brushed away dust, then produced an apple from within the long red cloak he was wearing. He split the apple in two with his sharp but clean fingernails and offered half to the boy. Larten wolfed down the fruit. When Seba saw how ravenous the child was, he gave him the second half of the apple too. Taking it with a brief nod of thanks, Larten sat crosslegged like Seba and munched down to the core, chewing the pips and all.

"I am guessing that you have not eaten in a while," Seba noted drily. "I would give you more if I had any, but I do not. You can hunt with me later, or I can bring food back for you if you prefer to remain where it is warm and dry."

Larten grunted and picked the remains of a pip from between two of his teeth. Squinting at Seba, he said suspiciously, "What do you want?"

"I do not want anything," Seba replied.

"Then why are you helping me? Why let me stay here and give me food?"

Seba smiled. "I am simply being hospitable."

"I don't believe you," Larten sniffed.

"You should never call a man a liar unless you are sure," Seba said coldly.

"You're living in a crypt," Larten said. "You can't be up to any good if you're staying in a place like this."

Seba raised an eyebrow. "I could say the same about you, young pup!"

Larten chuckled weakly. "I suppose you could."

"Why *are* you here?" Seba asked. When Larten's lips drew thin, he added, "You do not have to tell me, but you look troubled. I think you will rest easier if you are open with me."

Larten shook his head. "You first. What are you doing here?"

"I often stay in places like this," Seba said.

"You sleep in crypts?" Larten asked.

"Usually."

"Why?"

"Because I am a vampire."

Larten frowned. "What's a vampire?"

Seba was surprised. "You have not heard the tales? I thought, in this part of the world... Have you perhaps heard of the living dead? The walkers of the night?"

"Do you mean ghosts?"

"No. Vampires are…" Seba considered his words.

"Hold on," Larten said, a memory sparking somewhere inside his head. "You're not a bloodsucker, are you?"

"Now you have it," Seba beamed.

"I remember Vur telling me…" What? Larten only had a dim recollection. Vur had told lots of tales. It was something about creatures who drank blood and lived forever.

"There are many legends about vampires," Seba said. "Most are unreliable. We do drink blood to survive, but we are not killers. We do no harm to those from whom we feed."

"A monster who doesn't kill?" Larten was sceptical.

"Not monsters," Seba corrected him. "Just people with extraordinary powers. Or weaknesses, depending on how one looks at it."

Seba uncrossed his legs and stretched. "I cannot recall my exact age, but I am more than five hundred years old."

Larten grinned — he thought it was a joke. Then he saw Seba's expression and his smile faded.

"All vampires start life as humans," Seba continued. "We turn from the path of humanity when another vampire bloods us." He held up his hands and Larten saw small scars at the tip of each finger. "My master cut my fingertips, then his own, and pumped his blood into me. That is how I became a vampire."

"Why did he do it?" Larten asked.

"I wanted him to." Seba explained how vampires aged at one-tenth the human rate, meaning they could live for several hundred years. He told Larten of their great strength and speed, the codes of honour by which they lived. He explained about the hardships, the way humans feared and hunted them, how sunlight killed them after a few hours, their inability to have children.

Larten listened, entranced. Like most of his friends, he believed fully in a world of ghosts and magic, demons and witches. But this was the first time he had been exposed to the reality of that world, and it was far different than he'd imagined.

Seba told Larten some of the many myths about vampires. Crosses were meant to frighten them. Holy water could burn them. You had to drive a stake through a vampire's heart, then cut off his head and bury him at the centre of a crossroads to stop him rising again. They could change shape and turn into bats or rats.

"All rot!" Seba snorted. "The hysterical rantings of superstitious fools."

Larten had heard some of the tales before, but in relation to other monsters. He asked Seba if they were also real — demons, witches and the rest.

"Ghosts, yes," Seba said seriously. "And witches. As for demons and the like... Well, in five hundred years, *I* have not seen any."

He told Larten how he had been blooded as a child, and spoke of some of the countries he'd visited, and a few of the famous people he'd met. Larten didn't recognise most of the names, but he didn't admit that, not wanting to appear ignorant.

Finally, when Seba felt the boy had learnt enough about the world of vampires for one night, he reversed the question. "And you?" he asked gently. "Why are you here, so far from home and other humans?"

Larten's first instinct was to make up a story – he didn't want to confess to his terrible crime – but Seba had been honest with him and Larten didn't want to lie in return.

"I killed a man," Larten said hollowly, then told Seba the whole sorry tale. He cried while telling it. This was the first chance he'd had to think about what he'd lost, not just his best friend, but his parents, his brothers and sisters, his entire way of life. But he didn't let the tears overwhelm him. He kept talking, even when it hurt to speak.

Seba nodded slowly when Larten had finished. "From what you say, that wretch of a man deserved to be killed. Aye, and long before you struck the fatal blow. But murder always hurts. It is right that we grieve when we kill. If we did not feel pain, we would kill more freely, and what would the world be like then?"

"I'm evil," Larten moaned. "I'm going to hell when I die, or somewhere worse."

"A place worse than hell?" Seba smiled grimly. "That would be a bad place indeed! But I do not think your soul is damned."

"I stabbed Traz to death," Larten said, wiping tears from his cheeks.

"In the heat of the moment," Seba reminded him. "After he had slain your innocent friend. That is not the act of a vicious beast."

"You don't think it was wrong?" Larten whispered.

"Of course it was wrong," Seba said. "You took a life that was not yours to take and that should haunt you far into the future. But virtually all people do wrong at some point. The truly evil are those who willingly follow the path of violence when they find themselves on it. You have a choice now. You can embrace the darkness within you and become a monster. Or you can reject it and try to lead a good life from this night on."

"What if I can't?" Larten croaked. "What if I enjoyed killing him?"

"Did you?" Seba asked.

Larten shook his head crookedly, then sighed and nodded. "I felt powerful. He was bigger than me, and he'd hurt me – all of us – so much. Part of me wanted to kill him. After I'd stabbed him, I leant forward to poke out his eyes. I wanted to torture him, even though he was dead."

"But you restrained yourself?" Seba pressed.

"Aye. But it was hard."

Seba pursed his lips, impressed by the boy's honesty. "Vampires have a way of testing people," he said. "We do it before we blood humans. Great power must only be given to those responsible enough to deal with it. If we blooded the weak or craven, they would wreak havoc on mankind.

"We can taste evil in a person's blood," Seba went on. "It has a sweet tang. It should be vile and bitter, but evil often comes wrapped in sweetness. The test is not foolproof. We sometimes make mistakes. But in most cases it is accurate. I can test you if you wish."

Larten wasn't sure he wanted to be tested. If the result went against him…

"I will do you no harm," Seba promised. "If your blood is not to my liking, I will go my own way tomorrow and leave you be. Vampires do not judge humans or meddle in their affairs."

Larten gulped, then nodded hesitantly. He was afraid of what the vampire might reveal, but he'd rather know the truth about himself than live with uncertainty.

"This will hurt slightly," Seba said, taking the boy's arm. Using one of his sharp nails, he made a small cut just above Larten's elbow. As Larten winced, Seba put his mouth over the cut and sucked. For a worried second Larten thought he'd been tricked, that the vampire planned to drain him dry. But then Seba released him and swirled the blood around his mouth.

"Well?" Larten asked as Seba swallowed and narrowed his eyes.

"An interesting vintage," Seba joked, but Larten knew nothing about wine so he only stared at the vampire blankly. Seba licked his lips. "You have mixed blood."

Larten grew cold. "Does that mean I'm evil?"

"No," Seba said. "There is an underlying sweetness, but it is not overwhelming. I would say you are strong-willed, easily enraged, perhaps bent towards violence more than most, prepared to do bad things if provoked. Of course we already knew that, given how you acted today. But I do not think the evil strain is dominant. You will need to tread cautiously through life and guard your emotions carefully if you wish to master them. But in my opinion, you *can* choose good."

Larten was relieved but troubled. After today's violent explosion, he wasn't sure he could make those good choices. He recalled the way he had licked his lips, the disappointment that the dark part of him had felt when he stopped short of stabbing out Traz's eyes.

"I will leave you now," Seba said, rising.

"Where are you going?" Larten asked. He felt panic at the thought of being left alone in the crypt. It wasn't fear of the dead, but fear that Seba might not return.

"I must hunt," Seba said.

"For blood?"

"No. I drank last night. A vampire only needs to drink a couple of times a week. Less, in fact, but we prefer to drink small amounts often, rather than large amounts rarely. We can control our urges more easily that way. I go to find food now — like all creatures, we need to eat."

"You'll come back?" Larten asked, trying not to sound desperate.

"This is my room for the night," Seba said evenly.

"If I did not care to share it with you, I would ask you to leave. Only a fool puts himself out of his own home."

Larten smiled and shivered. "Could you start a fire before you go?"

"No." Seba squatted by the boy. "We light fires on occasion, but we do not rely on them. A vampire must be willing to endure discomfort. If you wish to be my assistant, you will need to accept that. You can take off your damp clothes, but ask no more of me than that."

"Wait a minute," Larten snapped. "Who said anything about me being your assistant? I don't want to become a vampire."

"Really?" Seba purred. "Then answer me this — where else will you go? Who will accept one of the damned other than a family of the cursed? Where will a creature of darkness hide if not in the shadows of the night?"

"*Damned?*" Larten echoed faintly. "I thought you said I wasn't..."

"I use the term poetically," Seba said. "In human terms, any killer is one of the damned. But vampires learnt long ago that we could find nobility in the depths of damnation."

Seba rose smoothly and surveyed the boy from a

height. "I will not force you. It does not work that way. Each person must choose freely, although not all of those who yearn to join are accepted.

"If you wish to chance the waters of vampirism, it will be many years before you can be blooded. First you will serve as my human assistant, travel with me, hunt for me, guard me by day, learn from me by night. In time, if you serve well, we can talk about blooding. We do not take anyone under our wing unless both parties are entirely sure that this is what the apprentice wants from life.

"But you must make your first decision tonight," Seba concluded. "If you wish to learn more about our ways, stay. If you think your path lies elsewhere, move on. I will be gone some hours. If you are here when I return, so be it."

He turned to leave, then paused and without looking back said, "You do not have to be alone. The world never inflicts loneliness upon us. That is something we choose or reject by ourselves."

With that, the ancient vampire slipped away.

Larten stared at the doorway long after Seba had departed, thinking of all he had been told. The day had seemed to stretch on forever and he was almost too tired to focus. But he forced himself to concentrate. He could tell that this was a moment of destiny. If he made the wrong choice, he would regret it, probably sooner rather than later.

Seba had said that Larten would have years in which to choose. He wouldn't be blooded until both of them were sure that this was the right thing for him. But Larten knew in his heart that the choice he made tonight would be binding. If he turned his back on humanity now, it would be forever.

Larten considered his future, thinking with wonder of all the things he would see and learn as a vampire's assistant, thinking with fear of all that he would leave behind. At first he worried about his other options. If he rejected the vampire, where would he go? How would he survive?

But as he thought on it more, he realised that didn't matter. This was all about choosing or not choosing one particular path. He needed to decide if this was the way for him. If it wasn't, he should leave the crypt immediately. Better not to start down a wrong path at all than head down it in the hope of making a detour when something better came along.

Larten wrestled with the problem some more, before ultimately deciding that he should go with what his heart was telling him. When he was satisfied with his choice, Larten shrugged off his clothes and sat in the darkness. His teeth chattered and he shivered wildly, but after a few minutes he figured that wasn't the way a vampire's assistant should behave. Straightening his back, he fought off the shakes and goosebumps and sat to attention, steady and calm, patiently waiting for Seba — his master — to return.

PART TWO

"Ladies and gentlemen — observe!"

CHAPTER EIGHT

The Wildcat sensed danger, looked around suspiciously and hissed. When there was no response, it lowered its head and tore into the remains of the rat on which it had been feasting. The Wildcat was a loner. Unlike ordinary cats, its kind had nothing to do with humans, preferring the open hunt of the countryside to the wretched scavenge of a town or village.

As the animal feasted, a shadowy figure moved up behind it. The predator slid along quietly, creeping ever closer.

The Wildcat's sense of danger kicked in again and it whirled. But it had reacted too late. The figure leapt and tackled the cat, grabbing it by the neck and twisting its head. As the doomed creature yelped and thrashed, its attacker pinned its neck with a knee, then jammed two hands into the beast's mouth. The Wildcat tried to chew the fingers, but it was in a hopeless situation. It resisted for a few seconds, then its jaw and snout were torn apart and it was all over.

Larten Crepsley knelt beside his kill and wiped his hands clean on the grass. He regarded the Wildcat with grim satisfaction. Vampires could not drink the blood of cats, but once fully bled and cooked, the carcass would provide a fine meal. Larten might struggle with the tough meat, but Seba's sharp teeth would easily tear through it.

Knocking the rat away, Larten hoisted the Wildcat on to his shoulder. It was heavy, but he walked without a stagger, whistling as he made his way back to the ruined castle where his master was sleeping.

It had been nearly five years since Larten first spotted Seba on the wall of the crypt. Larten had grown by several inches, and although he hadn't thickened out much, he was muscular beneath his dull brown shirt. Most youths his age would have struggled with the cat, but Larten had carried heavier in his time, always without complaint.

It was a cloudy but mild evening. It would be dusk soon and Seba would rise an hour or so later. The elderly vampire enjoyed a lie-in. He often remarked to Larten that when you'd lived for five hundred years, there was little in the world that seemed worth getting up early for.

They had made base in the ruins of an old castle three nights ago. Seba had not said why they were stopping here, many miles from the nearest village, and Larten hadn't asked. He'd learnt never to casually question the ways of his master. Seba had no time for lazy enquiries. He expected Larten to observe and learn, and query him only when an answer was worth seeking. Needless questions more often than not earned Larten a cuff around the ears.

Larten smiled as he scrambled over the rocky remains of one of the castle walls. Seba's occasional blows were nowhere near as rough or unjust as Traz's had been. The vampire could have knocked Larten's head off with a single punch, so he was always wary of doing damage. He had never truly hurt the boy, merely stung him. Even Larten's mother had hit harder than Seba Nile.

Seba was resting in what was once the main fireplace. The chimney had fallen in many years ago and created a sheltered niche. Larten had made his bed nearby, in the open, so if anyone came he could prevent them from stumbling across the sleeping vampire.

Larten hung the corpse of the Wildcat from a hook in a wall. He slit its throat and left it to bleed, then used bits of flint to start a fire. They often ate their meat raw, but a cat needed to be cooked or its blood would poison Seba.

Larten had relished the last five years, even the cold, wet nights when he'd had to bite into the horrible flesh of a live rat. He'd never once regretted his decision to become Seba's assistant. This was a hard life, but it was all he craved. He was still human, and many of the vampire ways were a mystery to him, but there was no question in his mind that this was his fate.

Though Seba was a thoughtful master, Larten's education was by no means easy. Vampire assistants had a much harder time than their masters. Though Seba made allowances for his human aide, he was a superior creature of the night. He was stronger, faster and more enduring than any human, and his assistant had to keep pace. If Seba marched all night, Larten wasn't allowed to fall behind. If Seba wrestled a bear, Larten had to pitch in and help.

Many assistants perished horribly before they could be blooded. That was the vampire way — they only accepted the most resilient. If you failed, the clan was better off without you. Larten knew he could expect no sympathy if he came up short of his master's expectations. Nor would he ask for any.

As the sun dropped, Larten slit the Wildcat down

the middle, then speared it on two spits and hung the meat over the fire. The smell was delicious, but he tried not to take pleasure from the scent. If Seba caught the young man's mouth watering, he'd probably toss the carcass aside and insist they hunt for raw meat.

As Larten tended the roasting cat, he hummed a song that Seba had taught him. It was an ancient melody, not of the vampires, but from the human world of three hundred years ago. Larten would have liked to learn a few vampire tunes, but Seba said they were best kept for the Halls of Vampire Mountain.

Larten grew wistful as he thought about the legendary home of the clan. Seba hadn't told him much about the mountain, but Larten had heard enough to fire his dreams. In his imagination it was a majestic place full of noble vampires. Great deeds were recounted there, lavish feasts were laid on for the Princes and Generals, and vampires had the opportunity to test themselves against their fellow night-stalkers. There was little in the human world to really challenge a vampire, but in the caverns and tunnels of Vampire Mountain you could truly find out what you were made of.

Larten stopped humming and kept his gaze on the roasting cat. He appeared to be listening to the crackle of the flames, but he was actually concentrating on very soft steps behind him.

"Will you be dining with us tonight, sir?" he called without looking up from the fire or turning around.

Someone clapped. "Very good," the stranger said, stepping forward out of the shadows. "You have a sharp ear."

"For a human," Larten murmured and turned to greet the visitor. He'd known by the sounds that their guest was a vampire — he moved the same quiet way Seba did when he was testing Larten's senses. If a vampire wished to sneak up on a human, they could move so silently that detection was impossible. But this one had wanted to give Larten a chance.

The vampire was about Seba's height but a little broader. He looked even older than Seba and had long white hair and a tight grey beard. He was missing his right ear. The flesh around the hole was a pale pink colour.

"Your name?" the vampire asked, approaching the fire and warming his hands.

"Larten Crepsley. I serve Seba Nile."

"Aye," the vampire said. "I gathered that much. I'm Paris Skyle. Seba has told you about me?"

"No, sir."

"Good. I don't like being discussed behind my

back." The vampire winked, then ran a curious eye over the young man's face. "Have you been with Seba for long?"

"Close to five years," Larten answered.

"Still a ways from being blooded then?"

"Seba doesn't say so, but I suspect that I am."

Paris sniffed the fumes from the cat. "In answer to your first question, yes, I accept your offer of dinner. But in future you should be more careful who you extend an invitation to. Never ask anyone to break bread with you unless you're sure of their intent."

"I knew you were a friend," Larten said. "Seba has been waiting for you. He didn't tell me, but I guessed."

"He might have been waiting for an enemy," Paris growled.

Larten shook his head. "You don't smile when you're waiting for an enemy."

"Certain vampires do," Paris disagreed, but was prevented from going any further by the appearance of a yawning Seba Nile. Paris yelled a greeting when he saw Seba drift from his sleeping quarters, and the vampires gripped each other's forearms, grinning widely.

Larten was excited – this was the first vampire he'd met since becoming Seba's assistant – but he fought to keep his emotions to himself. If he smiled the way the pair of old friends were smiling, he would earn a cuff from Seba. So, maintaining a neutral expression, he stayed by the fire and focused on the roasting Wildcat, acting as if that was his only concern in the world.

CHAPTER NINE

Seba and Paris ignored Larten for a long time, but he didn't mind. He could tell they were old friends who had a lot to catch up on. He served them their meal and provided wine from a jug that he'd bought in the last town they'd visited, then settled back and listened as they swapped tales and discussed other vampires.

"I lost my ear at the last Council," Paris told Seba. "I was surprised you were not there."

"I broke my leg on the way," Seba grunted, blushing slightly. "I had to hole up in a cave for five months. I fed on bats and the occasional stray goat. I thought my time had come, but I healed and was able to hobble out in the spring."

"I thought you had a bit of a limp," Paris laughed.

"Tell me more about your ear — you look strange without it."

Paris shrugged. "I was wrestling. My opponent's

nails caught on my ear and rather than take the time to free them, he ripped his hand away."

"Painful?" Seba asked.

"Aye. But I bit a chunk out of his cheek in response. We forgave each other over a mug of ale later."

Larten knew a bit about the Council. It was held every twelve years in Vampire Mountain, and vampires from all over the world made their way to it. Laws were passed there, tournaments were held and friendships were forged or renewed.

While listening, Larten was stunned to learn that Paris Skyle was one of six Vampire Princes. There were three classes of vampire — thousands of normal bloodsuckers, hundreds of Generals, and overseeing them all, the Princes. They held complete power. Their word was law.

Larten had pictured the Princes clad in fine costumes, like royalty in the stories he'd heard about as a child. He'd assumed they travelled with servants and guards. But apart from a few extra wrinkles, Paris looked much like Seba. His clothes were worn and dusty from the road. He was barefoot. He carried no crown or sceptre. And unless his retinue was hiding somewhere nearby, he was alone.

Paris threw away a bone and nodded at Larten to

serve up more of the Wildcat. He certainly had a princely appetite — this was his third helping.

"What's wrong with your hair?" Paris asked as Larten gave him the last chunk of cat. Though Larten's hair had dulled slightly since his days in the factory, it was the same unnatural orange colour it had been five years before.

"Dye," Larten said self-consciously.

"You dye your hair orange?" Paris chortled.

"The dye seeped into his skin years ago," Seba said. "There is nothing he can do about it."

"Why in the name of the gods did you dye your hair in the first place?" Paris asked.

"It was not by choice," Larten answered quietly. "I worked in a factory. This is how the foreman marked me."

Paris studied the boy some more as he chewed. "It's been a while since you took an assistant," he said to Seba.

"It is a complicated process these nights," Seba scowled. "I preferred it when you could snatch a baby from its cradle and no one cared. Now the Princes complain when we do that. They urge us to only take those who will not be missed by humans, and gods help you if you blood the wretch before he comes of age."

"Times are changing," Paris noted. "For the better, I feel. It's good that people worry more about their young, that we cannot pick as freely as we once did."

"Perhaps," Seba said grudgingly. "But such cautious manoeuvrings are not for me. I have trained and blooded several fine vampires over the centuries. In terms of bolstering our ranks, I have done more than my fair share for the clan."

Paris waved a hand at Larten. "Yet here you are with another apprentice."

Seba smiled. "Master Crepsley was an unusual case. When you find a boy eating cobwebs in a crypt in the middle of the night… well, such a lad has already driven a wedge between himself and the human world. If I had not claimed him for the clan, some other vampire surely would have."

"It sounds like an interesting tale," Paris murmured. "I will ask you to tell it to me one night, Larten. In return I'll tell you a few of mine if you're interested."

Seba laughed. "The lad does not know much about you, Paris, but in years to come, when he realises what a treasure trove of stories you are, he will remind you of that promise. You may live to regret it."

"Nonsense," Paris sniffed. "I never tire of discussing my great exploits."

Talk moved on and Larten was again forgotten. He had enjoyed being part of their conversation, even for a brief while, and looked forward to the time when he was considered worthy of full inclusion in talks between vampires as old and wise as these two.

Paris started to tell Seba of his recent adventures in a jungle. He seemed to have travelled to every country Larten had heard of, and many more besides. Larten was fascinated, but he excused himself and went in search of food to serve to the vampires later in the night. His duties had to come first.

Larten often hunted by himself. He hadn't in the first few years, but Seba had trained him well and now he was left to his own devices most nights. While he enjoyed hunting with Seba, he preferred the solitude of the solo chase. He'd never feared the dark as a child, but had been wary of it. Now he'd grown to love it. Humans retired when the sun went down, leaving the world in the control of the creatures of the night.

Larten wandered freely, relishing the heady smells, the sounds of small animals rustling in the bushes, the cries of owls and bats. While his senses were nowhere near as sharp as Seba's, he had learnt to see, hear and smell more than most humans ever did. He was aware of a different world unravelling around him, nature rolling its dice as it did every night, animals fighting, birthing, feeding, dying. There were a dozen dramas unfolding everywhere at once: in the bushes, the trees, beneath the soil. Larten could only follow a few of them — he saw an owl swoop on two mating mice and carry them away, and watched a fox drink by a stream, studying the water as if admiring its reflection. But the snatches he caught put a smile on his face like no human tale of ghosts and gods ever had.

On a rough road he kept to the shadows as a caravan of people passed, no more than three or four feet away from where he stood. It pleased him that he could follow their progress without them knowing he was there. He could have boarded the caravan and stocked up on fruit, meat and wine if he'd wished. But although he and his master sometimes stole when needs dictated, vampires were not natural thieves. They would rather hunt.

Returning to the forest, he became part of the hunting and killing frenzy. In a stream he caught two fish with his bare hands. Vampires could not drink the blood of a fish, but as with a cat, its flesh could be eaten once properly prepared and cooked. Larten kept one of the fish but gutted the other and left it lying on the bank as bait. He lay in wait nearby, as patient as any other predator. A rat nibbled at the guts, but Larten was in no mood for rodents, having eaten more than his fill of them over the last few nights.

Finally a stoat wandered by, homed in on the fish and greedily dug in. Larten gave it a minute, then swept down on the stoat and made short work of it. While washing his hands, he darted after another fish – this one even bigger than the first two – but it slipped away and made for the safety of deeper waters. Larten bid the fish luck as Seba had taught him – "Always respect the ones that get away" – then returned to the ruined castle with his catch.

Seba and Paris were arguing when he got back. Rather, Paris was shouting at Seba, while the slightly younger vampire was smiling wryly.

"This is the honour of a lifetime," Paris huffed. "Thousands of vampires dream of such an offer."

"I would say it is more than most even dare dream of," Seba nodded.

"You could enforce your views," Paris said. "If you object to the way we treat those who blood children, you could help reshape our laws."

"But I do not want to," Seba said. "I am old-fashioned. I do not like some of the changes that have been introduced in recent decades, but I acknowledge the need for change. I am no revolutionary."

"I need your support," Paris pressed. "There will be a crop of new Princes this century. I'm currently the second youngest, but at six hundred I won't be for long. The prospect of sitting beside a handful of young, headstrong Princes troubles me. I need an ally who sees things my way, but who can also relate to the newcomers. You're the best of both worlds, Seba, the old and the new."

"You flatter me," Seba murmured. "I am proud that you think so highly of me, but..." He spotted Larten listening. "Paris has made me a marvellous offer, Master Crepsley. He has pledged to help me become a Prince."

"A Vampire Prince!" Larten gasped, eyes widening. He didn't know much about Seba's past. He thought his master was a General, but he wasn't certain. And even if he was, Larten figured he couldn't be one of great importance, since he had so little to do with the rest of the clan.

"At least the boy is excited by the prospect," Paris muttered sourly.

"Power always impresses the young and foolish," Seba said dismissively.

Larten scowled at his master and almost snapped at him, but bit down on his tongue, not wanting to earn a thrashing in front of their visitor. "How do you become a Prince?" he instead asked Paris Skyle.

Seba frowned — he would have preferred Larten to listen some more before chipping in with questions — but Paris was happy to answer.

"A General is nominated by an existing Prince," Paris explained. "If his fellow Princes approve — one can object, but no more than that — it's put to the vote. That can take a few years, because at least three-quarters of the Generals must be asked. If the majority give their backing, he's invested at the next Council."

"But what do you have to do to be nominated?" Larten pressed.

"You must prove yourself worthy," Seba cut in. "It starts with knowing when to ask questions and when to be silent."

"Peace, old friend," Paris laughed. "I have irritated you. Don't take your anger out on the boy."

"I am not angry," Seba said. "I am amazed and humbled by your offer. But I must ask you not to take this further. If you do, I will have to publicly reject you and that would be embarrassing for both of us."

"I don't understand," Paris growled. "You deserve this. You're respected by everyone. If you were the power-seeking sort, you could have swung a nomination a couple of hundred years ago."

"But I do *not* seek power," Seba said quietly. He

stared into the flames of the fire and spoke in a quiet tone that Larten had never heard him use before. "I fear true power, Paris. I have seen it twist people, change them beyond recognition. Some, like you, thrive on it and remain masters of their souls. But I do not believe that I would be one of those.

"There is much about the clan that I would change. I would have us regress to a simpler, purer way of life. I think we interact too much with humans. I dislike the Cubs and their war packs. I do not approve of the impasse between ourselves and the vampaneze. I would push for less personal freedom, more regimented control of ordinary vampires by the Generals, a tighter, more restricted community."

"What's wrong with any of that?" Paris asked. "I feel that way myself."

"But you can act neutrally," Seba said. "You can balance your personal wishes against those of the many. You are happy to make suggestions, but not impose your will. You consider both sides of most arguments.

"I could not. My emotions would get the better of me. I do not trust myself to act as selflessly as a Prince should. Please, Paris, do not tempt me. Some are fit to rule, but I am not one of them. If I accepted the power of a Prince, you would live to regret it. More importantly, so would I."

Larten was bewildered by his master's words. He had always thought Seba was in total control of himself, the equal of any challenge. It distressed him to think that Seba was afraid. The vampire had been urging Larten to overcome his fears for the last five years. How could he now back away from his own like this?

"The boy is disappointed," Paris remarked, spotting Larten's expression.

"Larten is sharp, but inexperienced," Seba said stiffly. "He may see it my way in time. Or he may not."

"If he doesn't, I certainly do." Paris laid a hand on Seba's arm and smiled, then arched an eyebrow at Larten. "Wipe that look from your face!" he thundered. "An assistant should never dishonour his master, even by thinking poorly of him."

"But… you said… I thought…"

"I think Seba is incorrect," Paris said. "He would be a fine Prince, a credit to the clan. But I can only judge him by what I see. He judges himself by what he feels. We should all be so honest and true to ourselves. It takes a vampire of the highest integrity to acknowledge self-doubt. My respect for Seba has increased after our talk tonight. Yours should too."

Talk turned to other matters. Larten listened for a while, then slipped away and idly explored the forest. Thinking back over everything he'd heard, he wondered who or what 'war packs' and the 'vampaneze' were — both terms were new to him. But mostly he pondered Seba's rejection of power and tried to decide how that made him feel.

Paris had gone when Larten returned. The boy looked around in case the Prince was still in sight, but he and Seba were alone.

"Most vampires do not bother with farewells," Seba said without looking up. "We live for so long that after a time we tire of saying goodbye. Do not take it as a sign of disrespect."

Larten thought his master was avoiding his gaze because he was ashamed. But when he edged around the fire and caught Seba's wistful look, he realised the vampire's thoughts were elsewhere.

"You wish you had accepted," Larten said softly.

Seba nodded. "Part of me craves power." He smiled bitterly and glanced at his assistant. "But it is a part I do not like, a part I must always be wary of. I said you had mixed blood when I tested you, Larten. What I did not tell you was that I have it too. My master almost rejected me when he tasted my blood. But in the end he gave me a chance. He is long dead, but there are not many nights when I do not think of him and vow to honour his memory by denying the hunger of my lesser self."

Seba sighed and fell silent. Larten quietly cleaned around the elderly vampire, quenching the fire, scattering the ashes, bagging the remains of the Wildcat.

Finally Seba stirred. "Did you notice Paris's bare feet?" he asked.

It was an odd question, but Larten was accustomed to strange queries. "Yes. I assumed that was his preference."

"No," Seba said. "Some vampires disregard footwear as a matter of course, but Paris is not one of them. He has commenced his trek to Vampire Mountain, to attend the latest Council. When we undertake that trip, we cast our shoes aside and travel barefoot. It is one of the rules of the clan."

"Are you going to the Council this time?" Larten asked.

"Aye," Seba chuckled wryly. "Broken legs permitting."

"And…" Larten hesitated.

"… will I take you with me?" Seba shook his head. "Human assistants do not make the trek. You must be at least a half-blood."

"You're leaving me behind by myself." Larten wasn't dismayed. He would be able to get by for a few months without the guiding hand of his master.

"I *am* leaving you," Seba said, "but not by yourself. There is a reason why I have not cast aside my shoes yet. I wish to make a detour before I set off. An old friend of mine is travelling nearby and I think you will enjoy his fine company." The old vampire smiled warmly. "Tell me, Larten, did you ever hear tales in your youth of the weird, wild and wonderful *Cirque Du Freak?*"

CHAPTER TEN

Gervil was on fire. Flames engulfed his lower legs, his hands, his torso and his face. People in the crowd were screaming. Some had fainted. A few fled by the exits at the back of the large tent. On the small stage, Gervil writhed, fell to his knees and rolled around as if trying to quench the flames.

A couple of the braver men tried to mount the stage and rush to Gervil's aid. But as they clambered on to the boards, the owner of the Cirque Du Freak, Mr Tall, appeared before them suddenly. It was as if he'd materialised out of thin air.

"Please return to your seats, gentlemen," Mr Tall murmured in his deep, croaky voice, his lips barely moving. "Your efforts are appreciated, but unnecessary."

The men stared doubtfully at the impossibly tall, bony man in the dark suit and red hat. He had huge hands, black teeth and even blacker eyes. They'd seen him at the start when he introduced the show. He had looked merely strange then, eerie in appearance, but otherwise harmless. Now, staring up into his pitch-black eyes, the men felt uneasy, as if the tall owner of the fantastical circus was peering into their hearts and could stop them with a whistle if he wished.

"The Cirque Du Freak has been touring the world for more than three hundred years," Mr Tall muttered, and even though he spoke softly, everyone in the tent heard him. "We have lost several audience members in grisly circumstances during that time — as I told you before the show began, this is a place of fabulous dangers and we cannot guarantee your safety. But in all those years we have never lost a performer. And we will not break that fine record tonight. Observe!"

Mr Tall stepped aside and the people in the crowd saw that Gervil had stopped struggling. He was sitting in the middle of the stage, still covered in flames, but grinning. He waved at the stunned spectators, jumped to his feet and took a bow. As they realised this was part of his act and went wild with applause, Mr Tall slipped off stage and paused out of sight of the audience, where Larten was watching, mesmerised as he had been every time he'd seen Gervil in action.

"A lively pack tonight," Mr Tall said. "But I think they will be quiet after this." He studied the toys and sweets on the tray that Larten was holding. He picked up a statue of Gervil and frowned. It would stay lit for more than a month once its owner set it on fire. That was impressive, but Mr Tall wanted the flames to last for a year. He walked off with the statue, stroking the side of his cheek, considering the problem. Larten barely noticed. He was entranced by the real Gervil, who had now brought a woman on stage and was letting her set his tongue on fire.

Larten had been travelling with the Cirque Du Freak for six weeks and he still found himself transfixed at each performance. Tonight's show had started normally enough. After Mr Tall's introduction, a group of scantily clad dancing ladies had taken to the stage, to the delight of the men in the audience. Mr Tall didn't like the dancers – he felt they cheapened the show – but they were expected. By the end, nobody would remember them — they'd stream away yammering about Gervil, Laveesha and the rest. But many had come to see semi-naked ladies, and Mr Tall knew that it paid to give your audience what it wanted. At least to begin with.

Rax, the human hammer, followed the dancers. He could hammer nails into wood and stone blocks using his head. It was a fun but unspectacular act. Merletta, a magician married to Verus the Ventriloquist, followed Rax. She was a skilled magician and wore almost as little as the dancers, so she was warmly received. But, like Rax, she offered nothing out of the ordinary.

Gervil was the first of the magical freaks. His appearance marked the real start of the show. The lucky people in the crowd would be taken on a voyage of dreamy, unbelievable dimensions from this point on. By the time they filed out an hour or so before midnight, their imaginations would never be the same again.

The hairless Gervil could set his flesh on fire and not be burnt. It was a truly remarkable gift. Larten knew that many people came to the Cirque Du Freak convinced it was a sham. And while they fell into a wondrous spell during the performances, he was sure a lot of them would convince themselves in the cold light of day that it had all been a clever act.

Larten knew better. He had travelled with these people, eaten with them, run errands for them, traded tales with them. Each performer was genuine. Mr Tall had no place in his show for fakes.

Gervil finished by setting his eyeballs on fire – that part of the act still shocked Larten – then left the stage to riotous applause. There was a break after that, during which Larten wove through the crowd, selling wares from his tray, shaking his head with a smile whenever he was asked how Gervil had endured the flames.

Salabas and Laveesha were the stars of the second act, Merletta sandwiched between them in order to allow the crowd to draw its breath. She often performed in all three acts, a variety of impressive tricks. She had amazed with playing cards to begin with. Now she displayed her escapology skills, wriggling free of chains and shackles, topping it off with an escape from beneath a dropping frame of stakes. Her routine was slick and exciting, but nothing compared to the pair set either side of it.

Salabas Skin looked like an ordinary person. He told a short story about his life and made it sound very dull. "But then, one day, I had an itch. I tugged at my skin and lo and behold…" He grabbed the flesh of his right forearm and pulled. The skin stretched away from the bone as if it was made of some supple fabric.

To gasps of disbelief and delight, Salabas proceeded to stretch the skin all over his body. He pulled out the wall of his stomach by nine inches on either side. Tugging the flesh of his face, he invited audience members up and had them attach more than fifty pegs to his cheeks. He tied the skin of his chest into a bow.

His grand finale involved Salabas gathering the skin

of his throat. He raised it higher and higher until it formed a weird mask over his mouth and nose. It was both disgusting and hilarious. Salabas exited to a huge round of cheers, as he did every night.

Laveesha was billed as the tattooed lady. Most freak shows had a tattooed performer, someone who showed off their fleshly display of art, but Laveesha's tattoos were mystical and spellbinding. They changed shape whenever somebody sat close to her and stared at them. The inks would shimmer and run, break apart, then reform to reveal a new image, reflecting a hidden desire or secret of the person watching.

Laveesha always warned her volunteers of the power of her tattoos, and urged them not to come close if they had any deep, dark secrets they wished to hide from the world. Killers had revealed their murderous deeds in her presence. So had other criminals. Many more had brought forth the faces of people they lusted after, or images of loved ones who had died.

Her show was unsettling and upsetting. Yet volun-teers always came, even after the first few had reeled away from the tattoos in tears or screaming or protesting their innocence. They were drawn to her, compelled to approach, darkly fascinated by what their souls would reveal. It was like having a mirror that showed only the features you least wanted to behold. A person might hate such a mirror, yet still feel driven to stare into it.

Laveesha could have entertained a steady stream of customers all night, but she stopped after the sixth. She was a superstitious woman and didn't like a straight string of seven clients. But as she took her bows, a number of people slipped away to meet her in her tent for a private audience. Individuals sought out Laveesha after every show, even though she never offered her services or told them where her tent was. Larten could have eavesdropped on those meetings, but he didn't, partly because it would have been rude, mostly because he was scared of what he might learn.

He circulated with his tray during the second interval. Dolls of Salabas Skin disappeared from it like magic — they always sold well, especially the versions which you could eat. But although there were beautifully crafted dolls of Laveesha, featuring a variety of tattoos, Larten only sold a couple of them. If he had been responsible for production of the merchandise, he wouldn't have bothered with any doll of Laveesha. But Mr Tall made most of the sweets, toys and dolls, and for him the reward lay in the creation more than the sales.

"Having no need for money, I would happily give

my wares away," he'd told Larten one day, "but humans don't appreciate anything unless they pay for it."

Larten had noted the tall man's use of the word *humans*, but made no comment. There was a lot more to Mr Tall than met the eye, but the owner of the Cirque Du Freak guarded his secrets carefully and Larten figured he would learn more by watching than by asking questions.

Acrobats spun around the stage while Larten and his team sold goods to the crowd. Most of the acrobats doubled as the dancing ladies at the start, only now they were dressed in different costumes. Once they'd departed, a couple of clowns caused chaos in the aisles, drenching people with water and telling rude jokes. Mr Tall was a master when it came to judging the mood of an audience. Laveesha was a true star, but she had a grim effect on the crowd. These simple entertainers were his way of shifting the show back on track for an uplifting finale guaranteed to send everyone away with a smile. (On other occasions he kept Laveesha back until the end and sent the audience away uneasily into the night. He liked to experiment with the line-up.)

As the clowns rolled away, fighting and cursing, Verus the Ventriloquist took to the stage. He started with a dummy, like any other of his kind. But after a few minutes he put the wooden figure aside and pointed at a woman near the front.

"I think you have been secretly admiring me, madam," he said.

The woman looked shocked and opened her mouth to protest. But what came out was, "Yes, Verus, you're the most dashing man I've ever seen."

Her husband started to roar at her, but his angry cry changed halfway through and instead he said, "I've been admiring you too, Verus!"

The crowd erupted with laughter as they realised Verus was manipulating the pair, working them as he had the dummy. The laughter never stopped as Verus picked on one member of the audience after another, having them say whatever he wanted them to, but in their voices, not his.

As Verus drew his act to a close, Merletta came on one last time. Verus cocked an eyebrow at her, but she shook her head. He focused and pointed both hands at her. He was trembling slightly. Merletta only smiled, then crooked a finger in Verus's direction. He fell to his knees and declared, "You're beautiful, Merletta! You're the real star of the show!"

To a chorus of cheers and whistles, Verus rose and passionately kissed Merletta before exiting the stage.

In real life the ventriloquist and magician were married, but they never told that to an audience. It was more fun to let people think that Merletta had turned the tables on Verus.

After a few small tricks, Merletta sawed a woman in half, then made herself vanish. Mr Tall came on with the final performer, Deemanus Dodge. As the stage was cleared, Larten and others went through the crowd, handing out rotten fruit and vegetables, along with dirt-encrusted rocks and chunks of coal.

"Ladies and gentlemen — observe!" Mr Tall yelled, producing a bar of solid gold. A hush fell over the audience, all eyes pinned on the yellow bar. It was a genuine fortune. Though there were some wealthy people in the crowd, most were poor and had to scrape by in life, surviving day to day in a hard, cruel world. A bar of gold like this would change their lives forever.

"You have all paid an entrance fee and bought many of our trinkets, for which we bid you thanks," Mr Tall said. "But you do not have to go home lighter of pocket. We will give you a chance to win this gold bar and walk out of here rich beyond your wildest dreams. When I leave, Deemanus will issue a challenge. If any of you get the better of him, this bar will be yours."

Mr Tall glided off stage and Deemanus stepped forward. He was wearing a white suit and a matching bowler hat. He smiled at the silent, covetous crowd. "It's very simple, good ladies and gents. All you have to do is throw your missiles — that is to say, the objects that have been handed out — at me. You can throw other things too: shoes, coins, whatever you like. The first person to hit me wins the gold bar."

Deemanus stood there, smiling and waiting. For a few seconds nobody moved. Most people were frowning, trying to figure out the catch — winning a gold bar could never be *that* simple. Then one man, a bit quicker or greedier than the rest, stood up and threw a head of cabbage at the stage.

Deemanus stepped aside as the cabbage sailed past. "A lame first shot," he chided the man. "Surely the rest of you can do better than that."

As soon as he said it, objects rained down on him from all directions. People threw manically, savagely, fruit, vegetables, rocks and coal. Some tore off their shoes or snatched trinkets from their pockets and lobbed those at him. Many raced to the front of the stage for a better shot, tussling with those in their way. One over-eager man produced a gun in his furious excitement and fired two shots at the performer.

Deemanus dodged everything, even the bullets. He didn't move at an incredible speed, but simply seemed to dance around the stage, making tiny adjustments to his limbs to avoid the flying objects.

It seemed to last an age, but in reality the act lasted no more than a minute. The rain of objects trickled to a drizzle, then ceased. People were panting, wide-eyed, staring hungrily at Deemanus, scouring his suit for the slightest smudge. But it was spotless. He turned slowly, letting everyone see, even taking off his hat to display the top of it. Then, with a wink, he bowed and skipped from the stage.

Disappointment gave way to chuckles. People laughed at others and themselves, appreciating the humour in their wild display. A few looked genuinely bitter, but most had enjoyed the sport. The applause, as Mr Tall took to the stage to bid them goodnight, was deafening. They filed out in high spirits, buying more of the toys and sweets from Larten and his crew, before strolling home to catch as much sleep as they could before work early in the morning.

As the last patron left, Larten stowed his tray, then returned to the tent to help clean the stage. This was the only part he disliked, but with lots of people chipping in, they swept up quickly enough. By midnight he was sitting by a huge fire with the cast and crew of the circus, enjoying a hot drink and the warm glow of having been part of another legendary, unique and freakishly fabulous performance.

CHAPTER ELEVEN

Larten woke late in the morning and lay smiling up at the wooden ceiling of his caravan. He studied the rays of light streaming through a crack in the curtains. It reminded him of home, the mornings when he'd stirred before the others to catch the rising sun. But the memories didn't hurt. There had been times when Larten missed his family, and he still missed Vur. But many years had passed. He liked his new life and never looked back with regret.

Larten had a quick bath in a tub of chilly water out back. He shared the caravan with Verus and Merletta, and although the magician was easy-going in most ways, she was strict when it came to cleanliness. She insisted that Larten wash every third day. He had grumbled a lot to begin with, but now he didn't mind. After Larten had dried himself, he dressed and reported for duty. People were already dismantling the tent, supervised by Mr Tall. Larten helped stack and move chairs, then joined in the rolling of the canvas, an arduous but enjoyable task in which most members of the circus took part.

By midday everything was packed away neatly and the troupe took to the road in their horse-drawn carriages. Larten rode up front with Verus, enjoying the scenery from his seat beside the ventriloquist. Verus never forced words from the mouths of his friends — he kept his special talent for the stage. He was a quiet man at times like this, saying little, focused on the horse.

When Larten tired of the scenery, he withdrew and asked Merletta to teach him some tricks. He didn't have any freakish abilities, so he could never be a star at the Cirque Du Freak. But he had a quick hand and a keen eye, and was able to copy any trick once he'd seen it performed slowly. Merletta said he could carve out a career for himself as a magician if that was the path he wished to take. Larten knew he wouldn't – his heart was set on becoming a Vampire General – but it was fun to play at being a magician's apprentice.

Merletta ran him through a few of the card tricks that he'd already mastered, then taught him some new moves. He was able to slide cards around swiftly between his fingers and could make them disappear and reappear at will. Merletta was sure that he would soon overtake her in this discipline if he stuck with it. He was a natural at cards.

When it came to locks, chains and handcuffs, Larten already outshone his tutor. Merletta had never seen anyone pick a lock as swiftly or easily as the orange-haired teenager. There wasn't much she could teach him about escapology — once he'd learnt the basics, he had sprinted ahead of her.

Larten strolled between caravans later, visiting the friends he had made since linking up with the Cirque Du Freak. Some performers were vain and didn't mingle much — Gervil and Rax were especially pompous — but most were welcoming, as were the crew. Larten had never been more relaxed than he was here. If he hadn't felt the itch to explore the night, he would have been delighted to put down roots and call the circus home.

He wound up in Mr Tall's caravan. The owner of the travelling show was a solitary man. During their long hours of travel, he kept to himself. He didn't like physical contact with other people and hadn't even shaken Seba's hand when the vampire dropped off Larten. The pair were old friends — Mr Tall had received his visitor warmly and they'd swapped tales for hours — but the giant preferred not to touch those he mixed with.

Although Mr Tall didn't usually encourage visits, he had told Larten to call in on him as often as he liked. Perhaps it was because Larten was Seba's assistant, or maybe he had seen something in the orange-haired youth that interested him. Either way, the pair spent a couple of hours together most days.

Mr Tall was working on a Laveesha doll when Larten knocked and entered. The oversized man had enormous hands, but his fingers were even nimbler than Larten's. Using his fingernails and a tiny, sharpened piece of glass, he could make adjustments to a doll or statue that others could only see with the aid of a magnifying glass.

Mr Tall passed Larten a small set of jars filled with paint and he set to work on the pieces awaiting his attention. They often worked in silence like this, but on some days Mr Tall asked about Larten's past, or told him stories of Seba, Paris and other vampires. Larten always listened intently, absorbing every word, eager to learn anything that he could about the clan.

"Seba sends you his regards," Mr Tall said after a while. "He is doing well and has almost made it to Vampire Mountain. No broken legs yet."

The pair shared a chuckle. Even though he wasn't a vampire, Mr Tall was able to bond mentally with members of the clan. When two vampires bonded, one was able to find the other no matter where in the world they were. They could also trade basic messages. Larten didn't know how Mr Tall was able to bond with vampires, but he had no intention of asking. Mr Tall was even more secretive than Seba Nile.

"You hunger to follow in his footsteps," Mr Tall noted.

"Aye," Larten nodded, sighing happily at the thought of making the trek to the legendary mountain.

"It's a hard life," Mr Tall said. "Long, perilous, dark. You would have a much more rewarding career if you remained with us and worked on your stage skills."

Larten hadn't told Mr Tall about his lessons with Merletta, but he wasn't surprised that the circus owner knew.

"Why do you wish to become a vampire?" Mr Tall asked.

Larten paused, then frowned and admitted, "I'm not sure." It was a question he had never asked himself. He'd just followed his instincts since that first meeting with Seba in the crypt.

"Do the centuries appeal to you?" Mr Tall pressed. "Many humans yearn to lead long lives. Do you want to extend your natural time and live four hundred years... five hundred... more?"

Larten shrugged. "I'm not too bothered."

"Is it the power? You will be stronger than any human when you are blooded. You can force people to do as you wish, to respect and obey you."

"Seba..." Larten stopped. He'd been about to tell Mr Tall of Seba's decision not to become a Vampire Prince. But on reflection he wasn't sure if he should. That might not be something that Seba wanted to share, even with as close a friend as Hibernius Tall.

"Seba told me a vampire shouldn't seek power," Larten said instead. "We leave humanity behind when we're blooded. He said the Generals take a dim view of any vampire who tries to set himself up as a lord of humans."

"So why do you hunger to join the clan?" Mr Tall asked again and looked up. His gaze was dark and burning. Larten wanted to look away – he felt oddly afraid – but he didn't break eye contact.

"I don't know," Larten said. "It's just something I have to do. If I could explain it, I would, but..."

Mr Tall grunted. "A victim of destiny," he muttered and his head turned slightly as if he was sniffing the air. Larten realised that the caravan had come to a halt. Mr Tall always led the way, guiding his troupe from one place to another. He had a faithful piebald horse, but rarely sat up front to direct her. He was able to transmit his thoughts to the beast and steer the caravan from within.

Larten glanced out of the window. They had come to a crossroads. The horse had started to take a right turn, but now she hesitated, her head flicking to the left. To an outsider it would have looked like she was unsure of which path to take. But Larten knew that it was actually Mr Tall who was caught between two minds.

"There are some in life who serve destiny unconsciously," Mr Tall said softly. "Their lives are mapped out for them, but they are unaware of it. I envy their ignorance — I, alas, know far too much. Others make of life what they wish. They are free to choose and go this way or that on a whim. I envy their freedom — I, unfortunately, am bound never to make such a loose choice.

"I see the paths of other people sometimes." Mr Tall's voice was now a whisper and his eyes were distant. Larten wasn't sure if the tall man even knew that he was speaking. "I try not to, but on occasions I cannot avoid it. It's tempting to make a change, to interfere, to avert the pain that one can see lying in wait for others. Destiny is a tower of cards — nudge one just an inch and everything stacked on top comes crashing down. To be able to help people, but to live in terror of the dire consequences…"

Mr Tall's face darkened — his features seemed to vanish — then cleared. He smiled thinly at Larten. "Sometimes I think too much and say even more. Ignore me, my young friend. I should stick to what I am good at — running a freak show and carving dolls that nobody wants to buy."

As Larten stared at the mysterious owner of the Cirque Du Freak, not sure what to say, Mr Tall lowered his head and concentrated on the doll. Outside, the horse's head steadied and it took the right turn. Without hesitation it followed its original route, carrying Larten forward into the darkness and damnation of destiny.

CHAPTER TWELVE

Three nights later, Larten Crepsley took his first ever stage bow. Merletta sprang it on him at the last moment. He had been preparing his tray, and smiled briefly as Merletta approached, expecting her to pass him by. When she stopped, he looked up, slightly annoyed — she knew he was working to a tight schedule — only to almost drop the tray with shock when she said, "Would you like to be part of my act tonight?"

Larten thought he must have misheard. But before he could ask Merletta to repeat herself, she said, "You won't have to do anything hard, just wriggle out of some locks and chains. It will be easy. If you're not scared, that is."

She smirked, confident he wouldn't turn away from a challenge. But he nearly did, regardless of the shame it would bring.

"I can't," Larten gasped. "I don't have anything to

wear." Every performer had a specially designed costume.

"I'm going to plant you," Merletta said. "You'll pretend to be part of the crowd. I'll ask for a volunteer and pick you. That way you don't need a costume."

Larten tried to think of another objection, but Merletta headed him off at the pass again. "It was Hibernius's idea."

"Mr Tall wants me to go on?" Larten groaned.

"He thinks you have what it takes. I do too, though I wouldn't have introduced you to the act this soon. I'd have given you another month. But Hibernius thinks you're ready and he is rarely wrong in these matters."

"All right," Larten mumbled and set his tray aside. He didn't ask anyone to take it for him — he was sure Mr Tall would have thought of that and sorted it out already.

Larten took a seat in the tent and chewed his fingernails as the rows around him filled. He felt dizzy and sick. He would have backed out if it had just been Merletta, but he was certain Mr Tall was watching him. He didn't want to let down the man who had given him a temporary home.

When the lights dimmed and the show began,

Larten could hardly breathe. The first few acts came and went without making any impression on him — afterwards he couldn't remember what the line-up had been. He sat chewing his nails or squeezing his hands, praying to the gods for a miracle.

But Larten's prayers went unanswered and Merletta took to the stage as usual. She normally held back her chains for the second act, but mindful of what Larten was going through, she opened with them that night. She performed a few tricks, slipping free of handcuffs and knotted ropes. Then she stepped forward and asked if any young man would be so good as to come up and assist her.

A few dozen hands shot into the air — Merletta's beauty ensured that she never went short of lovestruck volunteers — but Larten's wasn't among them. He had made a spur of the moment decision to keep his hand down. Mr Tall might criticise him later, but that was better than having to get up there and…

To his amazement his right arm shot into the air and he half leapt out of his seat. He tried pulling his hand down, but he was no longer in control of the limb.

"There we go!" Merletta cried. "You'll do, young sir. Give him a warm round of applause, please, ladies and gentlemen. He's a brave young man, isn't he?"

As people clapped and cheered politely, Larten found himself edging forward, propelled, he was sure, by the magic of the unseen Mr Tall. About halfway to the stage he regained control, but it was too late to back out. Gulping, he mounted the steps and grinned crookedly as Merletta turned him to face the crowd.

There were so many of them! Larten had viewed audiences from the wings, and moved among them with his wares. But now that they were staring at him, he realised for the first time how tightly packed in they were. He saw hunger in their eyes — they wanted to be entertained and would be merciless if they were denied their sport. Their lives were short and hard. This was a rare chance to escape to a more fantastical world, and they would shower abuse on anyone who disappointed them.

As Larten's knees trembled, Merletta stroked his cheek and said, "I think he's shy." There were catcalls and some people roared at Larten to kiss her. He felt even more nervous now than he had felt in his seat.

As Larten thought about fleeing, Merletta grabbed his wrists and pinned them behind his back. He yelped as she snapped handcuffs on them and forced him to his knees. There were lots of cheers — the crowd liked it when their stars played rough.

"Will I make this young fool beg for freedom?" Merletta crowed.

"Yes!" the audience screamed.

"Will I make him crawl on his stomach like a toad and kiss my feet?"

"Yes!"

"Will I—"

"You'll do nothing," Larten snarled, snatching her arm and dragging himself to his feet. In his anger he'd picked the lock of the handcuffs and tossed them aside. Squaring up to Merletta, he steadied himself to deliver a foul curse. Before he could, Merletta gasped theatrically.

"I was sure I locked those cuffs," she called to the crowd. "Maybe there's more to this boy than I thought."

Larten hesitated as a few of the people — mostly ladies who felt sorry for him — clapped half-heartedly. He was glowering at Merletta, but he sneaked a sideways glance and saw that the hunger in the eyes of the crowd had been replaced with mild curiosity.

Merletta took Larten's arms and bent them behind his back again. But this time she was more gentle and he didn't resist. He kept still as she bound him with ropes and another pair of handcuffs, then turned him so that the audience could see.

"There," she exclaimed. "That will hold him." She

spun Larten so he was facing the crowd again. "Now what should I do with him?"

A few of the men shouted suggestions. As they yelled, Larten worked quickly, loosening the ropes and picking the lock. As Merletta considered the cries of the crowd, Larten slipped free, tapped Merletta on the shoulder and coughed softly.

Merletta gave a shriek, as if taken by surprise. Larten held up his hands and smiled. The audience applauded enthusiastically, accepting him as a performer. And the rest of the show flew by smoothly after that.

Larten felt like he was dreaming. He didn't want the act to end. He cherished every laugh and clap from the crowd. He wasn't up there with Merletta more than three or four minutes, but when he later looked back at this time and broke it down into every delicious second and thrill, it would seem to him as if he'd been on stage for an hour.

Larten relished his moment in the spotlight and couldn't understand why he had ever been scared. He had never been drunk, but he figured this must be what it felt like. It was as if he owned the world and could do no wrong.

Larten left the stage to a huge round of applause. The crowd had taken a liking to him and were pleased for his sake — they could see that he was a newcomer and that this meant a lot to him. Larten would never forget that wonderful feeling. It was a special moment in his life and he drew all the happiness from it that he could.

Mr Tall was waiting in the wings as Larten made his exit. The giant nodded to show his satisfaction. "You did well," he murmured. Larten beamed in response, his thoughts a hundred miles high. "But now you have a more mundane, but equally important job to do." When Larten frowned, Mr Tall angled his head to the left and Larten saw his tray, waiting on a table for him.

"Oh," Larten said, his smile fading slightly. "I thought…"

"No resting on your laurels around here," Mr Tall said. Larten had never heard that expression before, so Mr Tall translated it for him. "No sitting around on your backside. You had your moment of glory — bravo. I am pleased it went well. But you must not let yourself get carried away. There will be other nights and better performances, but now you must earn your keep. It is our way."

"Of course," Larten said, putting his childish disappointment behind him. He was glad Seba hadn't seen him act so vainly. Picking up the tray, he waited for the next act to finish, then wound his way through the crowd. He smiled when people said something nice or slapped his back, but he also stayed focused on his job and sold steadily, like a true professional.

There was a party later that night. They held parties regularly at the Cirque Du Freak. The celebrations served as a reward for the hard-working staff and stars, but they were also a chance for Mr Tall to invite influential people from the towns and villages near where they performed. While there was no law against a freak show (such restrictions would not come into play until the next century), life was easier if you kept a certain breed of man happy. It was better to flatter than annoy people with money and power.

Larten had always been shy at events like this. He normally kept to the sides, serving drink and food, avoiding conversation. But tonight he was on a high. It helped that some of the guests recognised him from his stint on stage and paused to commend his efforts. He even got chatting to a few young ladies, who smiled at him and shot him sly looks that the innocent boy missed completely. Larten was able to learn the ways of magic quickly, but it would be a long time before he learnt much about women!

He tried to sleep after the party, but he was agitated and couldn't keep his eyes shut. He kept flashing back to his time on stage, wishing he could have done more, trying to decide what he would do the next time he was up there.

Since sleep was proving elusive, Larten got up to watch the sunrise. He beamed as daylight crept across the world, warming the earth and waking the animals and birds. He considered going back to bed, but he knew he wouldn't be able to sleep. Besides, it had been a long time since he'd been abroad at so early an hour. It would be nice to go for a stroll and watch the world come to life.

Mr Tall had set up camp close to several towns and a scattering of villages. People would travel many miles for a performance of the legendary Cirque Du Freak, but the owner tried to make things as easy as possible for them. Larten skirted the homesteads, preferring the countryside. He smiled as he walked, as if the cattle and sheep he passed were old friends. He spotted a fox on its way home. He could have stalked and caught it, but there was no need — Seba would soon be feasting in the Halls of Vampire Mountain, and the cupboards and barrels at the circus were always well stocked.

Larten wove his way along paths and through forests for a few hours before pausing to rest. He sat on a hill overlooking a village and soaked up the sunlight. He was hungry, so he looked for a shop or inn where he might be able to buy food.

As Larten was studying the village, he spotted a handful of people scurrying towards a tiny church. A few more tore along after them less than a minute later. Larten's interest was aroused. This wasn't a holy day, and even if it had been, the people hadn't looked as if they were on their way to a service. They'd looked *scared*.

Larten trotted down the hill. A few more villagers hurried along and passed him on the street. None spared him a glance, even though a stranger would have drawn curious stares on any normal day.

He paused at the door of the church. He could hear angry muttering and weeping from within. He had a bad feeling about this. Perhaps it would be better if he didn't enter.

Larten would have retreated, except a family of four children and their parents pushed up behind him while he was dithering, the father carrying the smallest child and looking wild. "Go on!" the man snapped. "Get the door!"

Larten pulled the door open and stood back as the man and children brushed by. He still might have turned away if the woman hadn't waved him in. She looked on the verge of tears and Larten didn't want to upset her, so he stole in ahead of her and let her close the door behind them.

Larten's unease increased inside the church. He hadn't been in one since he'd become Seba's assistant. Vampires had their own gods, and although Larten didn't know much about them, he knew that he was finished with the religions of humanity.

But that wasn't the reason for his discomfort. He could see that these people were distraught. Many were crying. Others were cursing and striding around like caged wolves, snapping at their neighbours or the empty air.

A group of men stood at the centre of the church, in front of the altar, huddled close together as if protecting something. A few women and children approached them, but were turned back with angry gestures. Larten found himself drawn to the group as if hypnotised. It wasn't just curiosity. It was as if this church had been lying in wait for him, as if he had business here that couldn't be avoided.

The men close to the altar stared suspiciously at Larten as he drew near. He could see them silently debating whether to let the stranger step among them or drive him back like the other youths. Larten straightened his shoulders and looked directly at the men, neither slowing nor speeding up. As he came level, a couple shrugged and stepped aside so that he could slip between them.

Larten found a boy beyond the men, his own age or a bit younger. The boy was kneeling in the middle of four bodies – a man, a woman and two children – that were laid out on the floor, arms crossed neatly over their chests. The boy was rocking backwards and forwards, moaning softly, his hands outstretched and bloodstained. One lay on the forehead of the man. The fingers of the other stroked the cheek of the woman.

The man, woman and children were dead, and Larten could see that they'd been murdered — their throats had been slashed open. He also saw, by the small amount of blood around their necks and the pale shade of their faces, that their killer had drunk from them. No, even worse than that — they had been *drained*.

CHAPTER THIRTEEN

Larten was horrified. This looked like the work of a vampire. But Seba had sworn to him that the children of the night did not kill. He'd said that the Generals quickly put an end to any vampire who slaughtered humans without just cause. This could be the work of a mad, rogue vampire... or maybe Larten's master had lied to him.

The weeping boy was obviously related to the corpses — they shared the same build and facial features. The man and woman were his parents and the dead boy and girl were his brother and sister. Larten's heart immediately went out to the orphan. He knew how painful it was to lose those that you loved.

Larten was nudged aside as a man with long, grey hair moved forward for a better look. The man cursed, but didn't step back as others had. He wiped sweat from his cheeks, then cleared his throat.

"My Diana saw something pass our house this

morning, just before daybreak." A silence fell upon the men and all eyes focused on the newcomer. He looked nervous – he didn't like the attention – but he went on. "She was out back. A shadow passed in the dark. She said it looked like a man, but at the same time it didn't. She thought it was a monster. I told her not to be daft — kids are always imagining things in the dark. But when I heard about this…"

The man crossed himself. The boy was staring at the man now, his eyes starting to clear, fury filling the gap that grief left behind.

"Where did this *monster* go?" one of the other men asked.

"Towards Strasling's," the man said and a fearful sigh swept through the crowd.

The boy rose slowly, his gaze still fixed on the grey-haired man, who gulped and said, "Did you see anything, Wester?"

The boy shook his head. "I was sleeping in the shed. Jon had a cold and was snoring like a pig. I went to the shed to escape the noise."

"We should go to Strasling's," a woman cried from behind them. "Take crosses and stakes and…"

She fell silent when others glared at her. Larten was surprised by their reaction. He'd assumed the villagers would be eager for revenge. But as he glanced around, he saw that most were looking at the floor with shame.

"We all know why this happened," Wester said. He had a soft voice and there was a trembling edge to it, but he spoke clearly. "My da helped kill one of those beasts last year. We moved to a new home afterwards, in case any of its kin came seeking revenge, but they must have found us anyway. Ma tried to tell him we hadn't gone far enough, but he wouldn't..."

Tears welled in the boy's eyes and he stalled. People blessed themselves and muttered words of consolation. But nobody slid forward to embrace Wester or pledge their support.

"I've got to go to Strasling's," Wester said, brushing away tears. "I know if any of you come with me, and we kill this monster, another might come looking for you and your folk, like this one came for my da and us. I won't ask for help, but I'd appreciate it if anyone offers."

Wester stood over the bodies of his dead family, head low, awaiting a response. When nobody said a word, he nodded sadly and picked up a bag lying to the left of his father. "I'd be grateful if you'd bury them, and me too if you find my bones."

The boy strode through the ranks of men – they parted before him like a flock of sheep breaking ahead of a wolf – and marched up the aisle. He slipped out and closed the door softly behind him.

"We should help!" the woman who'd spoken earlier shouted. "If we don't, we're nothing but–"

"We know what we are!" one of the men roared. "You think any of us wants to let a child like that go off by himself? But Jess Flack interfered and look where it got him. If he'd left the monster alone when it came to his village, he'd be alive now, and his family too."

"We'll pray for him," another man said, moving to the altar. Larten realised this was the priest. "Maybe he'll find the strength to kill this thing and that will be the end of it."

The other men looked dubious, but filed back to the pews, joining their wives and children. Soon Larten and the priest were the only two standing. The priest smiled uncertainly at the youthful stranger and waved for him to step down. In response, Larten spat at the priest's feet. A shocked gasp ran through the church.

"You're nothing but cowards," Larten snarled, the words coming from a dark, angry place inside him. "I hope your animals die, your crops fail and that each one of you rots in the fires of hell." He felt the same sort of cold fury he'd felt the day he killed Traz.

As the church members gawped at him, Larten

considered adding a few curses, then decided against it and hurried down the aisle. Wester Flack had a head start. If he didn't catch up with the boy quickly, he might lose him — unlike the rest of the people in the church, Larten didn't know the way to Strasling's.

A couple of minutes later, Larten drew alongside Wester. The boy frowned warily at the orange-haired stranger.

"I'm Larten Crepsley. I want to help if you'll have me."

"Why?" Wester asked. "I don't know you. What business is this of yours?"

Larten didn't want to confess to being worried that the murders might be the work of a vampire like his master, so he told Wester the other — equally truthful — reason for his interest.

"You remind me of myself. I once went up against a foul murderer and nobody helped me. I had to face him all on my own."

"What happened?" Wester asked.

"I killed him."

Wester gulped, then said, "This is no ordinary killer. It's a monster. The beast is stronger and faster than us. I'll most likely die, and if you come with me, you will too."

"I'm not afraid of death," Larten said quietly. "And I've no family to worry about, unlike those cowards back in that church."

"It's not their fault," Wester sniffed. "The monsters don't pass through here often and never kill many when they do. But if you anger them…"

"This isn't the first time that it's happened?" Larten asked and Wester shook his head. Larten licked his lips and tried to make his next question sound natural. "Do you have a name for the monsters?"

"The old wives have lots of names," Wester snorted. "Most of us just call them bloodsuckers, because they drink the blood of those they kill." He cocked an eyebrow at Larten. "Still want to come with me?"

"Do you see me backing off?" Larten growled.

Wester sighed. "Forgive me. I don't mean to be rude, but I'm not myself. When I walked in and found them…"

Larten gave the boy's arm a squeeze, remembering what it had felt like when he lost Vur, trying to imagine how it must feel to find all your family murdered at the same time, to be the only survivor. His heart went out to Wester, and he swore a silent oath to do all that he could to protect this lonely, brave orphan.

"What's Strasling's?" Larten asked.

"A burnt-down mansion," Wester explained. "The man who lived there was evil. He practised dark magic and killed lots of people. The villagers say the house was struck by lightning and all within died by the hand of God. But I think a group of them torched it and drove back those inside when they tried to get out."

"Nice place you picked to come and live," Larten grinned.

Wester managed a weak chuckle. "We didn't have much choice. After Da helped kill the monster last year, we weren't welcome in our own village, nor any of the others. I think they only accepted us here because they still feel guilty about what happened in Strasling's."

"The monster your father killed," Larten said carefully. "What was it like?"

"I don't know. He never told us. But he took this bag when he went after it. I brought it with me from the house."

Wester opened the leather bag and Larten peered inside. He saw a hammer, a cross, a bottle of clear liquid that he guessed was holy water, some garlic, a small saw and three wooden stakes.

"The cross and holy water will hurt the monster, but not kill it," Wester said with the air of a person who'd done this a dozen times. "We need to drive a stake through its heart, then cut off its head, scoop out its brains and fill the skull with garlic. Then bury the body and head separately at the centre of a crossroads."

Larten nodded soberly, staring with fascinated horror at the implements. If he was right and they were on their way to confront a real vampire, the holy artifacts would be of no use, and the saw and garlic were superstitious extras. But a stake through the heart… aye, that would kill even the strongest of the so-called living dead.

"They sleep in the daytime," Wester concluded. "If we're lucky, we'll be able to kill the beast before it wakes."

"And if we're unlucky?" Larten asked.

Wester smiled without humour. "Then it will be a good time to make your peace with God, because you'll be seeing him soon."

CHAPTER FOURTEEN

The walls of the ruined mansion were scorched black from the fire that had destroyed it. There was still a foul smell in the air, although it had been years since the blaze. It felt like a dark, forbidding place, even to a night creature like Larten. It didn't surprise him that the monster – the vampire? – had picked this spot for its base.

They each took a stake from the bag. Wester kept the hammer. He gave Larten the cross and stuck the holy water in a pocket. He left the saw and garlic in the bag outside the ruins, telling Larten that they could return for those later if they were successful.

The scared boys slowly picked their way through the debris, saying nothing, studying each new room or corridor at length before entering. The roof and upper floors had fallen in, but lots of floorboards and tiles remained in certain sections, casting scores of shadows. There were many places for a sun-fearing killer to hide.

If Larten had been by himself, he would have waited until midday when the sun was at its strongest, then proceeded at a snail's pace, making as little noise as possible. But Wester was in a hurry to wreak revenge. He couldn't bear to stand still — he might go mad if he did.

Larten spotted the opening to the cellar. It had been half-covered by several planks. He considered saying nothing to Wester. It might be for the best if the boy never saw it, if he explored the rest of the ruins and came to the conclusion that the beast wasn't here. They could go home and that would be the end of it.

But Larten had come to uncover the truth, not engage in an act of deception. He was here to help Wester, not slyly direct him out of danger's way. The orphan deserved his shot at revenge. So Larten tugged Wester's sleeve and pointed.

Wester's cheeks paled. For a moment he looked like he might bolt for safety. Then he steeled himself, nodded grimly, led the way to the steps and pushed some of the planks aside.

They descended in silence and soon found themselves in a small cellar that had probably been used to store food and wine in the past. It was dark, but not pitch black. Light filtered through from the entrance behind them and also from cracks in the ceiling.

There was something lying by the wall to their right, in the darkest part of the room. It was the shape of a human, covered by thick blankets. Wester started forward, but Larten stopped him. Before advancing, he made a slow turn, studying the walls and ceiling. He had been taken by surprise once in a place like this — he wasn't about to be caught out twice.

Having checked for an ambush, Larten moved ahead of Wester and edged to one side, leaving clear the most direct route to the body. He would give Wester the first strike. If the boy failed, Larten would leap to his aid. He'd have been happier taking the lead — after his years with Seba, he was sharper than any human his age — but this was Wester's battle, not his.

As Wester closed in, Larten spotted a problem. Wester would have to pull back the blankets before striking, in order to pinpoint the beast's heart. That would give the monster a chance to defend itself. Larten slid in front of Wester. The boy hissed and raised the hammer and stake — he'd been so focused on what he had to do that for a moment he didn't realise it was Larten who'd stepped in his way. Then his vision cleared and he relaxed slightly.

Larten pointed at the blankets, then at himself, and made a gesture to show that he would pull them back. Wester nodded. Larten made another gesture, trying to encourage Wester to hammer the stake home quickly. Again Wester nodded, but he looked irritated now — did Larten think he planned to stand around and whistle a few verses of a song before he struck?

They came within touching distance of the blankets. Larten's hands were shaking, but he didn't mind — only a fool wouldn't be scared in a situation like this. He bent softly. He wanted to flex his fingers, but was afraid his knuckles might make a cracking sound and alert the sleeping monster.

Larten glanced up at Wester. The boy looked sick, but he wiped sweat from his brow, then positioned the stake over the area where he assumed the killer's heart would be. He lifted the hammer. Like Larten, he was shaking, but he had a firm grip on his weapons.

Larten grabbed the coarse, hairy fabric of the blankets and prepared to pull. But before he could, the blankets were tugged sharply by the shape beneath. Caught off guard, Larten was jerked sideways into Wester, knocking him over.

As both boys shrieked, the killer of Wester's family sprang to its feet and sneered at the amateur assassins. Even in the darkness of the cellar, Larten could see that this was no vampire, and for that small mercy he gave thanks — at least Seba had not lied to him. The creature's skin was a gloomy purple colour and its hair, eyes, lips and fingernails were red. It had the form of a man and dressed like one, but it was clearly no human.

Wester scrambled to his feet and swung his stake wildly. The purple-skinned beast chopped at the boy's arm. Larten heard bones snap and then Wester fell, screaming with pain. His stake dropped from his now useless fingers and rolled away.

The red-haired thing glanced at Larten and frowned when it saw his orange hair. It was momentarily thrown, not sure what to make of its strange assailant.

Larten seized the moment of indecision and threw his stake at the monster. The beast ducked and Larten lunged. He grabbed Wester's stake and came to his feet a safe distance from their opponent. As the purplish creature straightened and studied its foe, Larten fixed on the area around him, not on the monstrous man. He stood motionless, stake by his side, trying not to breathe.

Wester pushed himself off the floor and lashed out with his hammer. The killer caught it and calmly snapped off the head. As Wester stared despairingly at the piece of wood in his hand, the monster clubbed him over the head and he slumped. It was impossible to tell if he was unconscious or dead, and Larten had no time to worry about it.

The monster shifted away from Larten as it struck Wester. Larten was tempted to break for the stairs, but that was what the beast wanted. If he turned his back on the purple-skinned killer, he was finished for sure. So he held his ground, moving as little as possible, not blinking.

The monster faced Larten and narrowed its eyes, wary of this young but clearly far from foolish foe. The creature took a step forward, then smiled thinly and pounced, faster than the human eye could follow. But Larten had been trained to register the blur of a vampire. Seba had feinted at him on countless occasions, to sharpen his senses and teach him how to defend himself against an enemy quicker than he was.

As the killer lunged, Larten brought up the stake, judging it finely, trying to hit the spot where Seba would appear if this was just another test.

To his delight he struck flesh and the monster wheeled away, clutching its left arm. Larten had hoped to do more than just wound the creature, but at least this proved he had a chance. Adjusting his stance, he again focused on the area around him and waited for his opponent to make a second pass.

But the beast didn't move. It was smiling broadly, almost smirking. Licking a finger, it ran spit over the shallow cut on its arm and the wound began to close.

Seba's spit had the same healing properties. As far as Larten knew, that was only common to vampires. Confusion set in. Was this bizarre monster one of the clan? As Larten was trying to decide the nature of his foe, the killer spoke.

"You are a vampire's assistant. I could smell your master's scent, but I wanted to see you in action to be certain, hmmm?" The creature had an unfamiliar accent and an odd way of talking.

"What are you?" Larten snarled, not lowering his guard.

The beast frowned. "Your master has not told you about the vampaneze?"

Larten recalled Seba's meeting with Paris Skyle. Seba had mentioned something then about vampaneze. Larten had filed the nugget away, to investigate the matter some other time. It seemed that time was now.

"You have the speed and spit of a vampire," Larten said, "and you drink blood. But you're *not* a vampire, are you?"

"I'd rather be a dog than a vampire. I have no time for those of the *clan*." He spat out the word as if it was a curse. "I am of a purer breed. Vampaneze always drain our victims. We don't leech off them like your master."

"You kill every time you feed?" Larten gasped.

"It's the proper way," the vampaneze sniffed. "Vampires fed like us too, before they grew soft. We don't feed often — there's no need when you drink deeply — but when we do, we sup until we hit the bottom of the well, thus taking a shade of the victim's soul and honouring them."

"What are you talking about?" Larten asked.

The vampaneze tutted. "Your master has been lax. He should have told you that if a vampire drains a person dry, the vampire absorbs that person's memories, keeping part of their soul alive. We vampaneze kill every time we feed, but those we target live on inside us for decades or centuries to come."

"You think that makes it acceptable?" Larten snarled.

"Yes," the vampaneze said. "Vampires did too, before they grew soft."

Wester groaned and twitched. The vampaneze squinted at the unconscious boy. "He is one of the Flacks. I thought I'd killed them all. Generous of him to come to me like this. It would have been embarrassing if I'd left with the job half done, hmmm?"

As the killer stepped towards Wester, Larten slid between them. "Leave him alone."

"You're his friend?" the vampaneze asked.

"No," Larten said. "I only met him for the first time today."

"Then this is not your business," the killer snapped. "You're new to this, wet behind the ears, so I'm willing to overlook your interference. Vampires don't meddle with our affairs and we don't mess with theirs. I have the right to kill you for attacking me, but I'm prepared to let you leave. You can chalk it down to experience, hmmm? But the human dies. His father killed a friend of mine."

"Wester had nothing to do with that," Larten said, holding his ground.

The vampaneze shrugged. "In our world, the sins of the father are the sins of the sons. And the wife and daughters too. Last chance. Get out of my way."

"No," Larten said firmly. "If you want to kill Wester, you'll have to kill me first."

The purple-skinned man laughed. "So be it."

The vampaneze was even faster this time. Larten managed to strike, but his arm was slapped aside and a hard palm banged into his chest. He flew across the room and slammed into a wall. Stars flashed before his eyes, but he blinked them away and tried to haul himself to his feet. The vampaneze, having followed, stopped him with a soft shove to his head.

As Larten collapsed, defeated, the vampaneze squatted beside him. "Abandon the boy," he whispered. "If you renounce him, I'll spare you, yes, I will. Why waste your life on a worthless human that you barely know?"

"I gave him... my word... that I would... help," Larten gasped.

"But you cannot save him," the vampaneze reasoned.

"Then I'll... die with him. I gave... my *word*."

The vampaneze's blazing red eyes were terrifying, but Larten never lowered his gaze or flinched. Seba had taught him to face up to the things he was afraid of.

The vampaneze laid a jagged fingernail to the flesh of Larten's throat. Larten wanted to close his eyes and pray, but didn't. Instead he stared at his murderer, determined to die looking squarely at his executioner rather than cowering away from him.

The nail dug into Larten's flesh and he tensed, sure that this was the end. But then the vampaneze withdrew his finger. Wiping blood on his trouser leg, he stood and smiled tightly at the confused boy.

"You will make a true vampire," he said with grudging respect. "You'd fare better as a vampaneze – our way would suit a fiery pup like you, yes, it would

— but you've chosen your master and I won't ask you to break your pledge to him. But if you ever tire of the confines of the clan, seek me out."

The vampaneze cracked his knuckles, then spat at the unconscious Wester, the same way that Larten had spat at the feet of the priest. "I shouldn't have to leave, but if I don't, he'll come after me again and you'll have to help him — since you've given your *word* — and I wouldn't be able to pardon you a second time. Anyway, it's been a while since I ran beneath a full sun. The sunburn will be good for me. We should all suffer every once in a while, hmmm?"

The purple-skinned creature walked to the steps, where he paused and looked back at the startled Larten Crepsley. "I won't ask for your master's name, just as I have not requested yours. But I am not afraid to give you mine. When he asks, tell your master that *Murlough* held your life in his hands and chose to be merciful. Let him and his clan brood on *that* the next time they're belittling the good name of the vampaneze in the wretched Halls of Vampire Mountain."

With a sneer, Murlough bounded up the steps and smashed aside the planks at the top. He raced out of the wreck and across the fields, already wincing from the burning heat of the sun, looking for somewhere new to hole up and hide until night fell and the world was his again.

CHAPTER FIFTEEN

When Wester regained his senses, he was lying in the open, upstairs. He sat up, groaned and looked around with confusion. Larten was nearby. He'd thought about leaving, but he wanted to monitor the boy's recovery. Now he held a pouch of leaves filled with water to Wester's lips.

"What happened?" Wester asked once he'd drunk.

"The monster knocked us out," Larten lied. "He was gone when I recovered. I dragged you up here and went to wash my wounds and fetch water for you."

"He didn't kill us?" Wester frowned.

"Doesn't look like it," Larten laughed.

"Why not?"

Larten shrugged. "Who can know the mind of a monster?"

Wester staggered to his feet, groaning at the pain in his broken arm, and returned to the cellar entrance.

Larten tried to call him back, but Wester growled, "I have to be *sure*."

Larten lay in the sun while Wester explored the empty cellar. When the boy reappeared he looked drained of energy and life. He slumped next to Larten, his eyes full of tears.

"I failed," Wester whimpered.

"At least you tried," Larten consoled him. "We knew the odds were against us. We were lucky to survive."

"I wish he'd killed me," Wester cried. "How can I go back? They'll think I didn't face him, that I was afraid."

"Your wounds…" Larten muttered.

"Anyone can fake injuries," Wester snorted. He got up and looked around for footprints.

"What will you do?" Larten asked.

"Find the monster," Wester said. "I tracked him down once. I can do it again."

Larten didn't comment on how crazy that was — the vampaneze would already be many miles from here — but he said nothing. Wester would come to realise the futility of his quest in his own time.

"You won't be able to face him until your arm heals," Larten said, trying an indirect approach. "You'll need to rest, gather your strength, get a new hammer and more stakes."

Wester nodded thoughtfully. He tried moving his fingers and winced. "Do you know how to make a splint?" he asked.

"No," Larten said, "but I know a man who does. You should return to your home and bury your family. But if you truly don't want to," he said quickly before Wester could argue, "you can come with me and seek refuge at the Cirque Du Freak."

"What's that?" Wester asked.

"It's many things to many people," Larten said softly, taking Wester's good arm and leading him away. "For you, temporarily, it can be a sanctuary." But he knew, even as he said it, that what he was really offering Wester was a new home.

Wester's broken arm healed and so did the hurt inside him. The first few nights were horrible, a time of sobbing and hateful curses. Larten wouldn't have been able to console Wester by himself, but there were many at the Cirque Du Freak who knew what it was like to lose loved ones, to find yourself an outcast from the world. They did what they could to comfort the miserable orphan.

Wester was full of talk about how he was going to find and kill the monster. He made all kinds of outlandish plans. Larten listened quietly and never exposed the flaws in Wester's wild schemes, and as his fury dwindled, Wester came to see them himself and stopped muttering darkly. He hadn't forgotten his vow to slaughter the beast, and Larten doubted this was the end of the matter, but for the time being he was content to let it rest.

Even before he regained the use of his arm, Wester started helping Larten with his chores. He was intrigued by the magical circus. He worked hard and adapted swiftly to their way of life. Larten wondered sometimes if any stray in their position would fit in with the circus folk, or if he and Wester were different. He had a feeling the Cirque wasn't for everyone, only for those of a certain bent. Although they looked normal, he came to believe that he and Wester were in their own way every bit as freakish as the stars of the show.

The pair spoke often of their lives, especially at night when Verus and Merletta were asleep. In whispers, Larten told Wester about Vur Horston and Traz, how he had become a murderer on the factory floor. He thought Wester might think less of him then, but his new friend said nothing as Larten laid bare his soul, only listened silently and patted Larten's hand when he was finished.

Larten was less revealing about his more recent

movements. He let Wester think he'd been with the Cirque Du Freak for years. He didn't want to tell him about Seba and the world of vampires. If he did, Wester might make the link to the monster that had killed his family and maybe hate Larten as he hated the creature whose name he'd never learnt.

If Seba had returned in the middle of the night, when Wester was asleep, Larten would have left without waking the boy. He would have asked Seba if they could slip away quietly, and Seba, being old and wise, would surely have respected his assistant's wishes. That would have spared Larten the task of telling Wester the truth.

But Seba Nile returned without warning one evening, shortly before the start of a show. He tapped Larten's shoulder and when his assistant turned, the elderly vampire winked and said, "I hope you have not forgotten me already."

Larten cried out with joy – he'd missed Seba more than he realised – and threw himself into the vampire's arms, hugging him hard. Seba was surprised, but did not push the teenager away. Vampires were not as emotional as humans, but they were not entirely unfeeling. A rare display of affection was allowed.

"I will have your story soon," Seba said when

Larten released him. "I imagine you have much to tell me."

"And I'm sure you have even more to tell me," Larten grinned. They shared a laugh — both knew that Seba would tell his assistant next to nothing about his long trek and what he'd experienced at the Vampire Council.

"We will catch up with one another shortly," Seba said. "First I must find Hibernius and thank him for taking care of you." Seba caught sight of a boy hovering nearby, staring at them. He immediately sensed a connection between this stranger and Larten, but he didn't pursue it. Larten could tell him in his own good time, if he wished.

When Seba left, Wester nudged closer and asked, "Who was that?"

Larten sighed. "My master." He set his tray aside and faced Wester. "We won't be working tonight. There's a lot I have to tell you. About me... my master... and vampires."

Larten told Wester everything, how he'd first met Seba, his years serving as his assistant, what he knew about the clan, finishing with the truth about Murlough. Wester listened quietly, his face impossible to read. He was silent for a long time when Larten stopped. When he finally spoke, it was to ask, "Vampires drink blood, but they don't kill?"

"Aye."

"But you've only met a couple. How can you be sure?"

"Seba told me. I trust him. And Murlough confirmed it too."

"But he said that vampires used to kill."

Larten shrugged. "I don't know much about the clan's history. Maybe they were monsters like Murlough in the past. But they're not any more. From what Murlough said, there's no love lost between the two clans. He thinks vampires are weak for not killing when they feed."

"Have you drunk blood yet?" Wester asked.

"No. I'm still human. Seba won't blood me until we're both sure that it's right for me."

"If I thought that you were lying… or that Seba had lied to you… that vampires were in any way connected with what happened to my family…" There were angry tears in Wester's eyes.

"I swear on my life that vampires had nothing to do with that," Larten said, not breaking eye contact with the trembling Wester. "If you doubt me, I'll bare my chest and you can kill me now, drive a stake through my heart just as you meant to drive one through Murlough's."

"Very well," Wester said gruffly. "Wait here while I go find one."

Larten's mouth fell open and he gawped at the stern-faced Wester. Then he saw his friend's upper lip twitch and he punched him hard and cursed.

"You thought I was serious!" Wester hooted.

"Shut up," Larten growled.

"Are you always this easy to fool?"

"If you keep it up, I'll go find a stake of my own," Larten warned him.

Wester chuckled again, then sighed. "Will you leave the Cirque Du Freak now?"

"I suppose," Larten murmured. "I love the circus life, but I want to be a vampire more than anything. I can't say why. I just do."

"I think that I want it too," Wester said softly, stunning his friend.

Larten frowned. "You can't mean that. You didn't even know about vampires until I told you."

"You didn't know about them either before you met Seba," Wester countered.

"But our life is hard… there's so much to learn… you have no idea what you'd be letting yourself in for."

"Nor did you when you became Seba's assistant," Wester said. "I'll serve an apprenticeship like you. If I don't like it, I'll leave and maybe come back here. But

I *know*, the same way you knew that night in the crypt. I can't explain it. I just know it's the path for me. I think you do too. I think that's why you brought me here when you could have simply left me at Strasling's. It's maybe why you helped me in the first place."

Larten stared at Wester, troubled. Wester had as much right as he did to choose, but Larten felt protective of his orphaned friend. While he relished the challenges of the vampire life, he wouldn't wish the hardships on most folk.

Wester saw the indecision in Larten's eyes. It annoyed him – what gave Larten the right to choose for him? – but he hid his irritation and said, "I think this is fate. Would you deny me my destiny?"

Larten chewed his lower lip and shook his head. "It's not my decision to make. The choice is Seba's. But I will ask him, and put in a good word for you, if that's what you truly want."

It was, and later that night, after Seba had said his farewells to Mr Tall, Larten put Wester's proposal to him. The vampire studied Wester as Larten argued his case. The boy's eyes were steady and so were his hands. He had a calm, serious air that Seba liked. He saw potential in the boy. But he could see a problem too.

"There is one thing I demand of my assistants," Seba said. "*Truth*. Hold my gaze and tell me honestly — do you want to become a vampire so that you can track down and gain revenge on the vampaneze who killed your family?"

"That's part of it," Wester replied quietly. "I'd be lying if I said it wasn't. But it's not the whole reason. I want to be part of a community again. Part of a family. I could make a life for myself here at the Cirque Du Freak, but it doesn't feel right. When Larten was telling me of your people, your ways, how you embrace the night and honour it... My soul stirred."

"That is a poetic way of putting it," Seba smiled. "He has a fairer tongue than you, Master Crepsley." His smile faded and he refocused on Wester. "What if I told you to put all thoughts of revenge aside, if I said you could never seek vengeance, even if you ran into Murlough by accident one night?"

"I couldn't agree to such terms," Wester said. "He butchered my entire family. I can never forgive or forget that. I *will* seek revenge, either as a vampire or a human."

Seba approved of the boy's honesty. Wester had been open with him, and his thirst for revenge was justifiable. Even a General, bound by tighter rules

159

than most of the clan, had the right to kill a vampaneze who had slaughtered members of his human family.

"I have to test your blood," Seba said. "If it is pure, I will accept you."

Wester sat calmly as Seba cut his arm and sucked blood from the wound. Both youths watched silently as the vampire swirled it around his mouth. When he pulled a face and spat out the blood, Larten's heart sank. Wester's eagerness to become a vampire had taken him aback, but as he'd thought about it more, he'd warmed to the idea. Now it looked as if his master was going to reject Wester, and that hurt Larten more than he'd imagined it could.

Seba glowered at Wester for several long, threatening seconds…

…then winked. "Your blood is fine," he said. "In fact it is purer than Larten's or mine. I accept you without hesitation. You are my assistant now. Pack anything you wish to bring with you from this life. We leave in five minutes."

Wester and Larten shared a beaming glance. As they hurried off to fetch their belongings, Larten found himself thinking of Wester as he had once thought of a boy called Vur Horston — not just as a friend, but a brother.

PART THREE

"How many losses must I endure?"

CHAPTER SIXTEEN

Larten sat in the Hall of Khledon Lurt, sipping from a mug of ale, studying the red drapes hanging from the walls and ceiling, the statue of Khledon Lurt at the centre of the room, and of course the vampires. He had been here almost a week, but still felt out of place among the hardened creatures of the night. This was his first time at Council and it was hard to shake the feeling that he didn't belong.

He put his mug down and rubbed the scars on his fingertips, remembering the night when Seba drove his nails into the soft flesh. Larten had welcomed the pain because it meant he was leaving behind the human world, taking a step into the night from which there could be no return. He was proud of his ten scars, still shiny after all this time, but they didn't mean much here. There was a lot more to becoming a vampire of good standing than being able to show that you had been blooded, and

Larten was afraid he might not have what it required.

He was nearly thirty, so as a human he would have been in his prime. If he had battled his way up in the world of man, respect and security would probably have been his by now.

But he had been blooded as a half-vampire when he was eighteen, and as a full-vampire five years ago, so he looked like someone in his late teens. And all of his travel and experience paled into insignificance when compared with the adventures of vampires who had circled the globe countless times. Among these centuries-old beings, he felt like a child.

"There you are," Wester said, flopping down beside him and half draining a mug of ale. "Charna's guts! I needed that." The ancient curse sounded amusing coming from Wester, but Larten hid his smile, not wanting to hurt his friend's feelings.

"This place is amazing," Wester beamed. "So many tunnels and Halls. Have you been to the Hall of Perta Vin-Grahl yet? No, wait, never mind." He sniffed the air. "I can tell that you haven't."

"By implying that I stink, I assume you mean that the Hall of Perta Vin-Grahl is a bathing room," Larten said drily.

"Of a kind," Wester chuckled. "Make sure you bring

heavy clothes to wrap up in once you're done. They don't believe in pampering themselves here with towels or robes."

Wester drank more of his ale and looked around the cave, eyes sparkling. Wester and Larten had been blooded at the same time, but Wester hadn't become a full-vampire until two years ago. Larten had always been a faster learner, a few steps ahead at every stage of their training, but in spite of that Wester had adapted more swiftly to the world of Vampire Mountain. He had been mixing freely with other vampires since he arrived, learning about their history, exploring the maze within the mountain, making himself at home.

Larten had stayed close to Seba most of the time, saying little, not sure how to behave. Their master hadn't wanted to bring them to Council. They were young and he thought it would be better if they waited another twelve years. But they had argued fiercely with him and in the end he'd relented. At the time Larten thought Seba was worried about Wester, afraid that his slightly younger assistant wasn't up to the physical strain of the bare-footed trek through lands cold and hard. But now Larten had started to think that his master had actually seen a weakness in *him*.

Larten listened quietly as Wester told him of his

recent meetings, his new friends, what he'd learnt about life in the clan. After a while he lowered his voice and said, "I found out more about the vampaneze."

Both were intrigued by the mysterious, purple-skinned renegades – Seba had told them precious little of the other night clan – but Wester had more of a vested interest than Larten.

"A group of seventy broke away about five hundred years ago. There was a war. It lasted decades, vampires against vampaneze — they hated each other. In the end a peace treaty was agreed and there's been an uneasy truce ever since."

"I wonder why they sought peace?" Larten mused. "Why didn't they see the war through to its end and kill all of the traitors?"

"I haven't found out yet," Wester said. "But you know what this means?" Larten stared at him uncertainly. "Seba was alive then. He probably fought in the war."

"Perhaps that is why he never speaks of the vampaneze," Larten muttered.

"Aye. And maybe that has something to do with him not wanting to be a Prince." Larten had let that slip several years ago. He'd regretted it immediately and made Wester promise never to mention it to their master, but the pair had often discussed it in private, trying to figure out the secrets of Seba's past.

"Have you ever heard of Desmond Tiny?" Wester asked.

"No. Why?"

"A General mentioned him in passing when he was telling me about the war and its conclusion. I asked a couple of others about him. They got an edgy look when I mentioned his name, but they wouldn't tell me why."

"You think he was a traitor?" Wester had learnt that the names of traitors were never uttered by those of the clan.

"Maybe," Wester said, but he sounded unsure.

Further debate was ended when Seba entered the Hall and hailed them. Their master was with another vampire, a scruffy man clad in purple hides and no shoes. He was about Wester's height, but much broader than either of Seba's assistants. He had green hair, huge eyes and a small mouth. There were belts strapped around his torso and strange metal stars were attached to them.

"Larten, Wester, this is Vancha March," Seba introduced them, sitting down at the table.

Vancha nodded at the youthful vampires and called for a mug of milk. As one of the servants of the Hall handed it to him, he downed it with a deep gulp, then belched loudly and ordered another. Wiping his mouth with the back of a dirty hand, he smiled at Larten and Wester. "Seba's been telling me about you two. New-bloods, aye?"

"It has been more than five years since I was blooded," Larten corrected him.

Vancha laughed. "That's as good as new the way *we* measure time. Welcome to the clan." He pressed the middle finger of his right hand to his forehead, placed the fingers next to that over his eyes, and spread his thumb and little finger wide. It was the death's touch sign, something Larten had seen several times since coming to the mountain. As Vancha made the sign, he said solemnly, "Even in death may you be triumphant." Then he burped, called for a slab of raw meat and bit into it with relish. Larten frowned. He didn't approve of the older vampire's crude manner.

"Vancha is something of a traditionalist," Seba murmured as blood oozed down Vancha's chin.

"How old are you?" Wester asked, then raised a hand quickly. "No, let me guess, I'm trying to get used to this."

"Good luck," Vancha snorted. "I still can't tell how old most of these wrinkled prunes are. It depends on what age they were when they were blooded."

"I know, but it's possible to make an estimate..." Wester studied Vancha — pale like most vampires, with a scattering of small scars and wounds — and said, "Just over a hundred. Am I right?"

"Aye." Vancha was impressed. "I was delighted when I hit three figures. I don't think you can be considered a true vampire until you break the hundred mark. I've only recently started to feel like I'm a full member of the clan."

Larten smiled. It was the first time he had heard another vampire admit to feeling out of place. Despite his first impression, he found himself warming to the dirty, smelly Vancha March.

"What did Seba mean when he said that you're a traditionalist?" Larten asked.

"I don't hold with human comforts," Vancha sniffed. "Like vampires of the past, I have as little to do with mankind as possible. I eat my food raw, only drink water or milk — blood goes without saying — make my own clothes and never sleep in a coffin."

"Why not?"

"Too soft," Vancha said and laughed at the younger vampire's expression.

"Vancha is a throwback to a simpler breed of vampire," Seba said approvingly. "There were many like him when I was a child of the night. Most have died or adapted. Few have the strength or will to live as Vancha does."

"I'm not sure I'd call it strength," Vancha chuckled. "More like madness."

"Perhaps it has to do with your *mother*," Seba murmured wickedly and Larten was surprised to see Vancha blush.

Before he could ask any more questions, a vampire who didn't look much older than Larten or Wester approached their table. He had black hair and sharp eyes, and wore very dark clothes. If a raven took human form, Larten imagined it would look like this.

"Apologies, Master Nile, but my master would have a word with you."

"Of course, Mika," Seba said. "I will come to him shortly."

The vampire in black bowed, looked curiously at Vancha, then withdrew.

Seba sighed. "I knew that Lare would have a few chores set aside for me." Lare was one of the Vampire Princes. Larten hadn't seen any of them yet — they kept to the Hall of Princes most of the time. He wasn't even sure if Paris Skyle – the only other vampire he'd met before coming to the mountain – was at the Council. One Prince always stayed away, in case an accident befell the others.

Seba rose and groaned, rubbing the small of his back. "Vampires were not meant to live this long," he grumbled. "I should have gone to a glorious death at least a hundred years ago."

"Two hundred," Vancha said seriously, then winked.

"Prepare yourselves, gentlemen," Seba said to Larten and Wester. "The Festival of the Undead will soon commence. It is always an interesting time, especially for new-bloods."

"What does that mean?" Larten asked Vancha as Seba left.

"It means everyone will be looking to tackle you, to test what you're made of. It's a real baptism by fire — many newcomers never make it through the first night of the Festival." Vancha raised his mug of milk and smirked at the worried pair. "You'd better hope that the luck of the vampires is with you tonight, or I might be drinking a toast to your corpses in the morning!"

CHAPTER SEVENTEEN

The Festival of the Undead started at sunset in the Hall of Stahrvos Glen, more commonly known as the Hall of Gathering. Several hundred vampires were packed inside the cavern, dressed in their finest costumes. Even Vancha had washed and cleaned his hides. They were almost all men. Larten only saw a handful of women, and each of those looked as tough as any man.

There was an air of excitement in the Hall, but Larten and Wester were nervous. They sensed or imagined other vampires eyeing them up like a pack of wolves targeting a pair of lambs.

"Let's stick together when hell breaks loose," Wester muttered.

"Aye," Larten agreed. "We'll watch each other's back."

A gong rang loudly and all talk ceased. Larten stared with fascination as four Princes entered the

Hall and mounted a rough platform. He was pleased to see Paris Skyle among the royal quartet.

The other Princes were even older than Paris — one looked like he might be a thousand, though Larten knew that even vampires didn't live that long — but they moved easily and carried themselves proudly. Each would have to fight like any ordinary vampire this night, and if one was found wanting, he would not hold his post for long. Vampires had great respect for the elderly, but only if they could account for themselves in battle. The weak or infirm were expected to seek death as soon as possible.

"Welcome, children of the clan, and our thanks for travelling so far to be with us," the eldest-looking vampire, Lare Shment, said.

"The gods are surely proud of you all," the second, Azis Bendetta, smiled.

"As are we," Paris added.

"We hope you have concluded any pressing business," said the fourth and youngest of the Princes, Chok Yamada. "It's going to be challenges, tales of glory and mammoth drinking sessions for the next three nights!"

A huge cheer greeted that announcement.

"But before we run riot," Sire Yamada continued,

"let us hear the names of those who have passed on to Paradise since we last met for Council."

Each Prince took it in turn to mention a selection of the many who had died during the past twelve years. As each name was spoken, the vampires made the death's touch sign and murmured, "Even in death may he be triumphant." Lare concluded with the name of Osca Velm and a sad sigh swept through the Hall.

"Who was Osca Velm?" Larten whispered to Vancha.

"A Prince," Vancha said glumly. "I hadn't heard that we'd lost him. He must have fallen recently."

"We know Sire Velm's death is news to many of you," Paris said. "We held no ceremony for him because he didn't wish for one. He never believed that a fuss should be made over a bony old carcass."

Many laughed at that, but Vancha nodded gruffly. "I knew Osca. He would have hated a fancy funeral. He was a fine vampire. He knocked me flat once and broke three of my ribs."

As the sighs and muttering died away, Lare Shment clapped and said, "Let that be the end of our official business. We shall have no more until the Ceremony of Conclusion. Luck to you, my children."

"Luck!" the vampires bellowed with delight. And

even before the roars died away, mayhem erupted and spread through the Halls of Vampire Mountain.

Larten and Wester were swept along in a crush of crazed vampires. Their plan to help each other quickly evaporated as they were separated and left to fend for themselves as best they could.

The vampires were supposed to challenge one another in the gaming Halls, but several fights broke out in the tunnels on the way. For many of the clan, this was what they lived for, a celebration of brawn and bravery that came once every twelve years. It had been a long wait since the last Council and their lust for battle got the better of them. Nobody objected — such premature scraps were common. Their friends simply pushed them along or left them to wrestle in the dirt.

There were three gaming Halls. Several mats and roped-off rings catered for those who preferred hand-to-hand combat. In other areas you could fight with swords, spears, knives or any of a wide variety of weapons. There were wooden bars to balance on and rounded staffs to spar with, or ropes you could cling to while your foe tried to knock you loose.

Barrels of ale were in ready supply, as well as vats of blood. Larten hadn't thought to ask where the fresh blood came from. It had crossed Wester's mind a few nights earlier, but Seba had told him it wasn't the time to discuss such things. He'd said he would explain later.

Larten seriously thought that he was going to die. No vampire challenged him at first, but he received many wayward punches and kicks. One over-eager individual threw an axe. It missed its target and went swishing by Larten's head, skimming past his skull by only a couple of inches. He turned to swear at the clumsy oaf, then saw that it was Chok Yamada. Larten was new to many of the vampire ways, but he wasn't so naive as to openly curse a Prince!

As Larten raised a hand to salute the laughing Prince, a vampire slammed into him. Larten yelled with shock and spun to face a tall, ugly General with a nose that had been broken many times.

"First to three," the General grunted. Before Larten could ask what sort of a contest he was being challenged to, the General grabbed him by the neck, felled him and pinned his arms. "One to me," the General laughed, letting Larten rise.

Larten was prepared when the General attacked again. He tried to slip out of the bigger man's way and grab his arms, but the General read Larten's intentions. He slapped the young vampire's hands apart, wrapped his arms around Larten's waist, picked him off the ground, then smashed him flat and pinned him again.

"Try and make it interesting for me," the General sneered as a shaken Larten picked himself up and gasped for breath.

Larten swore and swung at the General's nose. The General twitched his head aside, caught Larten's arm and twisted it up behind his back. As Larten screamed, the General forced him to his knees.

"Beg for mercy," he growled.

Larten told him where he could stick his demand.

The General roared with laughter, then flipped the youth over and pinned him for the third and final time. He walked off without any parting comment, leaving a dusty, dazed Larten to stagger to his feet and glare at the floor with red-faced embarrassment. Around him, several young vampires jeered and applauded slowly, sarcastically.

Before the furious Larten could challenge those who were jeering, another vampire hailed him. "New-blood — come face Staffen Irve if you dare. Let's see what you be made of."

Staffen Irve wasn't much older than Larten. He was holding a club with a large, knobbly, metal ball hanging from a short chain at one end. He tossed a similar weapon to Larten and said, "Have you used these before?"

"No," Larten said, testing the club's weight and the swing of the ball.

"Then you better be a quick learner, boy," Staffen chuckled and took a swipe at Larten's face. If it had hit cleanly, Larten would have lost several teeth. But he was able to duck and the ball struck his shoulder instead.

Larten grimaced and lashed out. His ball bounced harmlessly off Staffen Irve's ribs. Staffen grunted and whacked Larten's shoulder again.

Larten lasted less than a minute. He fended off a few of the blows and managed to land a couple of his own, but when the ball smashed into his right leg just below his knee, he went down hard and was finished. Staffen pounded Larten's back a few times, hoping to goad him back to his feet, but when he realised the duel was over, he stopped and offered Larten a hand up.

"Not bad," Staffen said as Larten stood on one foot and squeezed back tears of pain. "You ain't the worst new-blood I've seen, but you'll need to put in a lot of work before the next Council."

The vampires who had been watching him laughed at that. To Larten they sounded like a pack of crows.

He would have liked to wade into them and tear their heads off, but the fight had been knocked out of him. Turning his back on those who had borne witness to his shame, Larten hopped away, trying hard to drown out their catcalls.

Staffen Irve's mild compliment should have given him hope, but Larten didn't think any amount of work would prepare him for the next Council or any after that. In his own eyes he was a failure. On the trek to the mountain, he had dreamt of winning every challenge and becoming an instant hero. While he knew that wasn't realistic, he was sure he would at least hold his own and not be disgraced. Now he knew better. He imagined more vampires laughing at him, the laughter following him as he limped away, and his head dropped ever lower.

One of the female vampires shouted at Larten and held out a long staff, asking him to duel with her. But the thought of being laid low by a woman was too much for him. It didn't matter that he wasn't meant to deny a challenge during the Festival of the Undead. He wanted out. Blushing furiously, Larten hurried to the exit and slipped out of the Hall, feeling smaller and more alone than he had at any time since he'd fled from the factory of silk worms as a scared young boy.

CHAPTER EIGHTEEN

The tunnels were littered with wounded or resting vampires. Larten didn't see any fatalities, but he was sure there would be several by the end of the Festival. No vampire would feel pity for those who fell. Humans might consider it a waste of life, but for vampires death in combat was the noblest way to die.

Larten didn't quite wish for death, but at least it would have spared him this indignity. He knew he was making things worse by hopping away – he'd now be seen not just as a weak new-blood, but one who ran when the going got tough – but he didn't care. All he wanted was to find a quiet spot for himself, so he could hide and nurse his injured leg and wounded pride.

"Hey!" someone called. Larten paused and looked around. Three young men were seated at a table in a niche in the tunnel, playing cards. The tallest of them was smiling invitingly. "Do you play?"

Larten blinked. "Why aren't you fighting?" he asked.

"Challenges are *so* eighteenth century," the vampire laughed, then extended a hand. "I'm Tanish Eul. Come and join us. Gambling is a far more civilised way to pass the time."

Larten stared at Tanish Eul and his companions. A bottle of wine stood on the table and another couple of bottles rested nearby. The men were dressed in the modern human fashion, hair carefully swept back. One even sported a monocle. They looked unlike any other vampire he'd seen.

Tanish Eul wiggled his fingers. "I won't hold out my hand forever."

Larten felt a great urge to join them, to share their wine and show off his card skills. He had a feeling they wouldn't care about his humiliation in the gaming Hall, that they'd laugh and make him feel like it wasn't important. He took a step towards the trio, then stopped. If Seba found him here, drinking and gambling when he should be fighting, Larten knew his master would be disappointed.

"Thank you," Larten mumbled, "but I have to go."

"As you wish." Tanish lowered his hand. "But feel free to drop in on us another time. You'll always find a welcome here."

Larten half-waved to the strangely dressed vampires and staggered away with a frown. After a while he stopped thinking about Tanish Eul and focused again on his battered ego. He had meant to rest in one of the more remote Halls, but as he limped down the tunnels, he just kept going. His feet almost had a will of their own. He came to a gate, ignored the stares of the disgruntled vampires who had been stuck with guard duty, and carried on down the maze of lower tunnels.

There were marks on the walls to show the way. He read them by the light of the glowing lichen that grew in most places here. At a fork he paused and considered taking a turn that wasn't marked, to lose himself and perish in a godsforsaken corner of the mountain. But as bad as he felt, he hadn't hit that low a point, or even anywhere near.

Finally he came to an opening and crawled out on to the face of the mountain. It was a gloomy night, the moon a thin arc in the sky, only a scattering of stars on display. Snow whipped around him and soon his orange hair was covered by a soft white cap. Ignoring the elements, he hopped down the mountain, wincing from the pain in his leg, but determined not to let it slow him.

After a while, Larten sought the shelter of a small

copse of trees. He was shivering and his clothes were soaked from the snow. Once he'd propped himself against a mossy log, he rolled up the leg of his trousers and examined the area around his knee. He thought a bone might have splintered, but he couldn't be sure. He wished this had happened to him on the way here. He would have had to miss Council if he'd broken a leg, as Seba had twenty-four years earlier. That would have been for the best.

There was a panting noise. Larten looked up sharply, eyes narrowing. His sense of vision had improved dramatically since he was blooded and he could see almost as clearly at night as he had in the daytime when he was human. Now he saw two wolves approaching, teeth bared, hackles raised. They looked like they might be getting ready to attack, but Larten knew it was just for show. They would bolt in a second if he made an aggressive move.

Larten whistled to the wolves. Their ears pricked and they whined softly, then came to him and lay by his side. He hugged the hairy creatures, absorbing warmth from their bodies. There was a bond between vampires and wolves – some thought that the clan had originally evolved from the beasts – but Larten felt especially close to them and most wolves responded to him eagerly.

The wolves, like the vampires, had come for the Council. They'd learnt long ago that there were rich pickings to be had – delicious scraps thrown out for them to devour – and dozens made the pilgrimage every time.

"I bet it's easier for you," Larten murmured. "If another wolf gets the better of you in battle, you just roll over and show your throat. He leaves you alone after that. A brief moment of humiliation, then you get on with things. You don't have to deal with scornful looks or jeers."

The wolves simply panted and lay at rest. Words didn't matter to them. They were accustomed to the prattle of the two-legged beings and coolly ignored it.

Larten lay with the wolves, silently brooding. Perhaps he would stay here for the day, then set off for the human world at sunset. Never return to Vampire Mountain or the clan. He could be a highly respected man in the normal world. His strength and speed would stand him in good stead. As long as he didn't seek too much power, the Generals would leave him alone.

As Larten considered a life of exile, the wolves raised their heads and snarled. Moments later Seba appeared, thrusting through the trees. One of the wolves rose warningly, then Seba whistled to it and the beast relaxed. Like his assistant, Seba had a special way with animals. Wester wasn't fond of the four-legged creatures, but Seba and Larten had often run and hunted with wolfen packs.

The wolves parted to allow Seba to sit beside his student, then shuffled up to him. Seba scratched behind their ears and told them how fine they looked. They panted happily and even let him examine their teeth.

Larten sat stiffly while his mentor was playing with the wolves. He feared a tongue-lashing from his master, but when Seba finally looked up, his eyes were clear and calm.

"I have been told of your defeats and how you stormed off."

"I didn't—" Larten started to retort.

"Did not," Seba stopped him.

Larten managed a weak smile. A few years ago he had told Seba that he wished he could speak like him — the elderly vampire always sounded very authoritative when he spoke. Seba had nodded seriously and said that he would train him.

"I *did not*..." Larten began again, but this time stopped of his own accord. The truth was that he *had* stormed off in a sulk. To deny it would be foolish. "You were right," Larten scowled. "Wester and I should not have come to Council. We were not ready."

"Of course you were," Seba said. "I never planned to leave you behind. I simply wanted the pair of you to think that coming here was your idea, not mine."

Larten blinked dumbly. "Why would you do that?"

Seba chuckled. "If you ever take an assistant of your own, you will find that they need careful handling. You and Wester often make *free* decisions that are actually entirely of my bidding. It is good for the young to think that they are in control of their choices, even when they are not."

Seba sighed and his smile faded. "But I am not the fine judge that I believed. I am to blame for your reaction tonight. I should have been harder on you in the past and made little of your successes in order to prepare you for your failures.

"I expect more of you than of Wester," Seba said quietly. "Wester will make a fine vampire if he does not die young in his pursuit of the vampaneze, but he lacks your potential. You have the capacity to become a vampire of great standing. Or so I believe.

"I have always tried to treat you the same as Wester, but I think I failed to hide my high opinion. You read my thoughts and, being young and impressionable, assumed that you were as noble and capable as I hoped you might become.

"I have been soft on you. Instead of setting you

tasks you could not complete, I played to your strengths and let you forge ahead. It is not a bad policy – most people need to build on a series of small successes, to increase their skills and give them a sense of self-belief – but it was the wrong approach in your case. You have grown headstrong and overly confident. Again," he said as Larten tried to object, "that was my fault, not yours. I let it happen because I was proud of you."

Seba leant against the tree and gazed at his student. "You thought you would crack many heads tonight, beat champions, set records, make a name for yourself, aye?"

"Aye," Larten said, smiling bitterly. "I know how foolish that was, but–"

"–you believed it anyway," Seba finished. "In my heart, part of me believed it too. I secretly hoped that you would take the clan by storm. That hope led me to misdirect you. I should have told you to expect the worst. You had never fought a vampire before. It takes time, practice and many losses before a new-blood can get the better of his peers. But because I believed that you could thwart those odds, I said nothing. That is why you have been hurt."

Seba got to his feet and rubbed his arms up and down. "I feel the cold these nights," he muttered.

"Perhaps I am not much longer for this world. In my youth I could sit through a freezing blizzard. Now..." The snow triggered a memory and Seba changed tack. "Do you know the story of Perta Vin-Grahl?"

"No. But Wester told me about the bathing Hall named after him."

"Perta was not much older than I when I became a vampire," Seba said, "but he was already an incredible warrior, destined for greatness. We all thought that he would become one of the youngest ever Princes.

"Perta passed into legend when peace was agreed between the vampires and vampaneze." Seba had a faraway, sad look in his eyes. "That was a terrible time. A lot of those who perished in battle were our bravest and best. For centuries arguments had raged. Vampires were once poised to become the dominant force of this world. There were tens of thousands of us, at a time when humanity was far less widespread and powerful than it is now. We could have taken control, made slaves of humans everywhere, become lords of all.

"The Princes led us away from that. They saw the perils of absolute power and convinced the clan that we would become dark beasts if we sought dominion. They urged us to withdraw from the affairs of man.

We made our base in lands no human would ever come to, and created laws to limit the influence we could exert over those who were weaker than us. Back then, vampires always killed when they fed, but the Princes outlawed those murderous habits.

"Many vampires disagreed with the new direction that we had taken. They felt that we had become vermin, sneaking around, stealing drops of blood here and there like leeches. Our numbers dwindled over the years. We no longer blooded as many assistants as we once did — there were new laws against it — and humans came to see us as prey. When we walked the world proudly and openly, no one hunted us, aware of the dire consequences if they killed a vampire. As we became more secretive, humans grew scornful of us, thinking us weak and cowardly. Vampire-hunting became a sport in many corners of the world."

"You think the Princes were wrong," Larten whispered, "that we should have stayed true to our original course."

Seba nodded slowly. "It was our natural way. We were predators, but we were not vicious. We killed when we drank, but we absorbed part of the human's spirit, so they lived on in a fashion. We were like lions — they are not evil when they kill, merely noble creatures of the wild obeying their fierce instincts."

Seba held up a hand as Larten tried to object. "Hold, Master Crepsley. I do not claim we should return to the old ways. We cannot. Too much has changed. I think we took the wrong turn at a key time, but now that we are on this path, we must go where it leads. I would like to make certain alterations and adjustments, but the vampaneze went too far and I would hate to see the clan follow suit.

"All of that is beside the point. I was telling you about Perta Vin-Grahl. He fought heatedly against the vampaneze when they broke away. Before they left, he was in favour of returning to the old ways. In arguments, he took the side of those who would go on to become the vampaneze. But he believed above all else in the need to remain united. He felt that change should come from within. He savagely opposed any move to split the clan.

"Perta despised the seventy vampires who turned their backs on us to establish their own order. He led the hunt to kill them. Many wanted to debate the matter with the newly formed vampaneze. They felt it was no more than a provocative gesture, designed to spark a response. They thought that the vampaneze could be tempted back into the fold.

"Perta knew that we had passed that point. He was determined to slay them all. He said that was the only way true peace could be achieved. If we let them live, they would return to haunt us. This was even before Desmond Tiny gave us the Stone of Blood and cast his dire prophecy."

"Who is Desmond Tiny?" Larten asked. "And what is the Stone of Blood?"

Seba waved a dismissive hand. "You will find out soon. You must go to the Hall of Princes before we leave, clasp the Stone and add your blood to that of the clan. I will explain it to you then.

"Perta killed many vampaneze. He lost a hand and half his lower jaw in battle – he could not eat solid food afterwards – but he kept going. He was the most accomplished, determined fighter I have ever seen.

"When a truce was declared, Perta could not accept it. There were others in his position, a group of angry, hateful Generals. They had lost friends and loved ones in the battles. They wanted to wage war against the vampaneze to the very end, even if it meant our end too. It looked as if there might be another split. We thought that Perta and his followers would break from us as the vampaneze had, to create a third brand of night-walkers and further weaken our position.

"But Perta did not wish to harm the clan. When he realised that he could not convince the majority to continue our war with the vampaneze, he gathered his followers and led them away. He took them to a place of ice and savage isolation. Some say it was Greenland, others the South Pole or somewhere equally remote. According to one of his followers who came back years later, they built a palace out of ice, dug tombs, finished off the blood they had taken with them, then lay in their frozen coffins and calmly waited to die."

Seba fell silent, thinking of the lost vampires he had known in his youth, recalling Perta's laugh and the flash of his blade. Once Seba had fought by Perta's side and killed three vampaneze, including the General who had blooded him when he was a youth, the one who had taught him as he taught Larten, whom he loved and respected above all others. That was the darkest night of Seba's life and he would never speak of it, not even now.

"The vampire who returned was insane," Seba sighed. "Lack of blood and the harsh elements drove him crazy. Who knows if his story of ice castles and tombs was true? Many vampires have searched for the burial place of Perta Vin-Grahl, but it has never been found and, even if it exists, I doubt it ever will be.

"But we know that Perta and his followers chose death instead of harm to the clan. Rather than lead his supporters to war with us, Perta led them away so that the clan could flourish. It was the ultimate sacrifice, made by a vampire of true greatness, one who put the wishes and needs of the clan before his own.

"There is a reason why I am telling you this," Seba said, eyes coming back into focus. "Perta was the finest fighter I have seen, beyond compare. He set many records at Council, defeating one challenger after another at wrestling, fencing, the bars. Everyone wanted a slice of Perta Vin-Grahl, to be able to say in years to come that they had faced him in his prime. He did not win every fight — nobody does — but he won far more than any other vampire in recent centuries.

"I remember the first time Perta came to Vampire Mountain." Seba smiled at the ancient memory. "He was skinny and dirty — Vancha March is a dandy compared to the young Perta Vin-Grahl! He had been blooded as a child but, like you, had never had much contact with other vampires until he came here. He challenged just about every General at Council that year."

"Let me guess," Larten sniffed. "He lost every fight, like I did."

"No," Seba said. "He was a tiger even then. He won most of the contests in which he took part. And those that he lost, he only lost narrowly, after a long, bloody fight.

"I mentioned that first Council to Perta many years later. I thought he would recall it with pride. But his face grew dark and he said he wished he had been beaten to a pulp. He said triumphing in so many challenges was the worst thing that ever happened to him."

Larten frowned. "Winning was bad?"

Seba nodded. "I was bewildered too, until he explained. A few years later, Perta was travelling with five young vampires. They looked to him as their leader and teacher, even though he had not blooded them. One of them hatched a plan to kidnap Lady Evanna and force her to bear children." He noted Larten's confusion and gestured impatiently. "That is a story for another time. Suffice it to say, the Lady of the Wilds is a great sorceress. You cross her at your peril.

"Perta was fearless and led his group against her. She fought back and killed all five of his companions. Perta escaped only because he was stronger and faster than the rest. She chased him for six months before one of the Princes begged for mercy on his behalf and convinced her to leave him be.

"Perta felt that he had the blood of those vampires on his hands. He had failed to consider their weaknesses. Having never tasted real defeat, he assumed nothing bad could happen to him or those who put their trust in him. That deadly encounter with Evanna taught him a costly lesson. But if he had tasted defeat earlier in his life, he would never have followed such a fatal course. Those five vampires might still be alive.

"It is good to be taught humility when we are young," Seba said softly. "If we do not experience pain as children, we will cause pain as adults. You have to learn from your beatings. Accept your shortcomings and work on correcting them, but welcome them too. You might one night be asked to lead others. If so, you must be able to see people as they are, not as you yourself might be. A true champion must know not only his own mind and heart — he must know the minds and hearts of those weaker than himself. You can only do that if you have stood where they stand."

Seba patted the wolves and smiled. "They are not so fast, these beasts, but they are strong. They can run for many miles and endure. We are not so different. It is hard for one so young as you to peer forward and focus on the centuries ahead of us, but I ask you to accept the word of one much older than you. Your losses now will profit you in the long run, *if* you learn from them, *if* you accept them and seek to rise above them for the right reasons."

"The right reasons?" Larten echoed.

"Come back and face Staffen Irve again," Seba said. "Ignore the jeers of those who mocked you. Wounded as you are, weaker and slower than Staffen, you should still challenge him and be defeated again, so that you can learn and grow."

Larten thought about that, then hobbled to his feet. "How long do you think it will take?" he asked. "How many losses must I endure before I can be a great warrior like Perta Vin-Grahl?"

Seba sighed — his assistant hadn't understood. This wasn't about overcoming one's limits, but acknowledging and living with them. He thought about trying again, but he felt either he lacked the right words, or else Larten was not yet ready to hear. Perhaps the young vampire had to learn his lessons the hard way, as Perta Vin-Grahl had.

"More losses than your ego can bear, less than your body can endure," Seba answered. As Larten puzzled over that, the elderly vampire clapped his assistant's back and offered his arm for support. With Larten leaning on his master, the wolves trailing close behind, the pair commenced the long climb back to the Halls of Vampire Mountain.

PART FOUR

"Now there's a man with style!"

CHAPTER NINETEEN

"Do it again."

Larten scowled and picked himself up off the forest floor. Flicking twigs and moss from his hair and clothes, he climbed the tall tree and edged out along a branch the width of his wrist. When he got as far as he could standing up, he bent, gripped the branch with his hands and kicked his feet into the air. It took him a few seconds to find his balance. Once he was steady, he walked out further on his hands.

"Stop," Seba said as the branch creaked and bowed from the weight. He was sitting higher up in the tree, chewing a bone. Wester was at the end of another branch, balanced on his hands like Larten.

Larten stared at the ground, feeling sweat trickle along his neck. Seba watched for a while, still chewing. Then, without warning, he tossed the bone in Larten's direction, but a couple of feet beyond the branch on which the young vampire was precariously perched.

"Catch it!" Seba barked.

Larten's left hand shot out and his fingers clutched for the bone. He almost made contact, but as had happened sixteen times already, his right hand shook wildly, he lost his balance and fell with a startled cry, hitting the earth not long after the bone.

Seba tutted, then said, "Do it again."

As Larten muttered angrily and climbed back up the tree, Seba dug another bone out of the bag in his lap, then threw it at Wester. His other assistant enjoyed no more success than Larten had and was soon picking himself up from the floor and wincing.

"This is ridiculous," Larten grumbled, staring at the branch with something close to hatred. "It is an impossible task."

"Not at all," Seba said. "Every vampire learns to do this. It is a basic test."

Larten squinted suspiciously at his master. There had been a lot of *basic tests* in recent years, ever since their visit to Vampire Mountain. Larten and Wester had failed most of them. He was starting to think that Seba was playing with them, setting goals that they couldn't possibly achieve. But why would he humiliate them in such a fashion? Maybe the tests were genuine and his assistants simply weren't up to the standards required of trainee Generals.

"I almost caught it that time," Wester said, joining them in the branches.

"No," Larten grunted. "You were nowhere close."

"Thanks for the confidence boost," Wester pouted.

"Are you *sure* this is necessary?" Larten asked Seba.

The elderly vampire shrugged. "The Generals are very demanding. They will test you in many ways. You must be flexible and experienced in a variety of skills. If you cannot do this, there is no point going any further with your lessons."

Larten sighed, shared a resigned look with Wester, then edged out along the branch for the eighteenth time.

Seba chewed a bone and watched neutrally. He waited until Larten was in position, then lobbed the bone at him, closed his eyes and waited for the thud. When it came, his lips twitched and he almost smiled. But when he opened his eyes again, there was no hint of a grin on his carefully composed face.

"Do it again."

Larten was in a foul mood when they made camp for the day. It had been a long, tiring night, but there was to be no rest for him.

"I would like a loaf of bread when I wake," Seba said

as he yawned and made himself comfortable. "Will you fetch one for me, Larten?"

"We are miles from the nearest village," Larten noted.

"I know," Seba said.

"I will not be able to catch much sleep by the time I travel there and back."

"You are young," Seba said. "You do not need a lot of sleep."

Wester wanted to volunteer to go instead, but Seba would be furious if he said anything. Assistants were never supposed to contradict their master.

"Do you want any particular type of bread?" Larten growled.

"Of course not," Seba said, settling back and closing his eyes. "You know that I am not particular."

"How about you?" Larten snapped at Wester.

"I'm fine," Wester said quickly.

Larten set off through the forest, grumbling and kicking any tree stump that got in his way. The last few years had been a frustrating drag. Endless tests, most of which he'd failed. No contact with other vampires. No adventures. Not much travel, and when they did go to a new country, Seba wouldn't let them explore. "I have already seen that," he would say whenever they asked to go sightseeing. "It is not worth the trek."

Wester was bored and irritable too, but he still had faith in their master. He believed Seba was doing this for a reason, that every vampire had to endure such treatment on their way to becoming a General.

Larten wasn't convinced. He thought maybe age had caught up with Seba, that his thoughts had become muddled. Maybe these weren't real tests at all, just ways to make his assistants look foolish. Nothing they did in recent times satisfied the grouchy old vampire. He found flaws in everything. Larten couldn't believe that other masters were this critical of their students.

He took his time walking to the village. He kept to the gloom of the forest as best he could, avoiding the rays of the sun, which were painful for him now. But sometimes he had to pass through a clearing. When he did, he raised his cloak — a tattered grey thing he'd picked up during his travels — over his head and jogged, muttering darkly once he was safely back among the shadows.

When Larten returned with the loaf — still warm, tucked away in the folds of his cloak — Seba stirred and called to him. "Is that you, Larten?"

"Aye."

"What took you so long?"

Larten bit down on his tongue to stop himself

cursing. "You said you were going to eat later. I did not think there was any rush."

"I am too hungry to wait." Seba beckoned impatiently for the bread. Larten resisted an urge to toss the loaf at his master's head, and instead unwrapped it and handed it across. Seba's eyebrows creased. "I wanted brown bread."

Larten trembled. "You said you didn't mind," he snarled through gritted teeth.

"Did I?"

"*Aye.*"

"Oh." Seba blinked innocently. "My apologies. I meant to ask for brown."

He held the loaf out to Larten and nodded in the direction of the village. Larten stared at the bread, wondering if it was possible to batter a person to death with it. Then he turned abruptly and headed back the way he'd come. He passed close by Wester, but his friend kept his head down, buried beneath a blanket, afraid Larten would vent his anger on him if he caught his eye.

Several weeks later, Larten and Wester were fishing. They stood in the middle of a fast-flowing stream, thigh-deep in cold water, hunched over. The test was to spear a fish with their little finger. It should have been a simple task, except Seba had tied a strip of cloth around their eyes so that neither could see.

"Listen closely, gentlemen," he called from the bank, where he was tucking into a pheasant that they had caught and roasted for him earlier. "No creature moves in complete silence. Focus. Train your ears. Ignore the sounds of the stream and the rumblings of your stomachs."

"Easy for *him* to say," Larten huffed, the delicious smell of the pheasant thick in his nostrils. He hadn't eaten since they'd arrived here four nights ago. Wester hadn't either. Seba had told them they could eat nothing until they caught a fish.

Wester bent close to the water and strained, but he could hear nothing moving beneath the surface, even with his advanced senses. After a few minutes he stabbed directionlessly, figuring if he did that often enough, he had to catch something eventually. But he came up empty-handed.

Beside him, Larten was struggling to control his rage. He was starving, wet and freezing. But worst of all, he felt like a fool. There was no way they could do this. If it was a still pond, perhaps, but there were limits to what even a vampire could do. Besides, when he'd studied the stream from the bank before getting in, he hadn't seen any fish.

Something bumped lightly against Larten's leg and he thrust at it. His nail struck true and he yelled with triumph. But when he ripped his blindfold away he saw that he'd only speared a piece of wood.

"You will not get fat on that," Seba chuckled, juices from the pheasant dripping down his chin.

"Charna's guts!" Larten roared and threw the stick at Seba. It struck the vampire's shoulder and bounced harmlessly to the floor. Seba stared at it, then at Larten, his expression unreadable.

"Apologise!" Wester hissed. He'd removed his blindfold and was trembling.

"For what?" Larten shouted. "He's treating us worse than animals. There's no way we can—"

"*He is*," Seba calmly corrected him. "*There is*."

"How about this?" Larten sneered. "*You are* a stupid, cruel, decrepit sham of a vampire!"

"Larten!" Wester gasped.

"*You have* lost your senses," Larten pressed on. He waded out of the stream and stood dripping before his master. "You *do not* deserve the title of General. You are setting us tasks that no vampire could complete, just to watch us fail. You should go and…"

He stopped. Seba had stood up and was heading for the stream. He got in and told Wester to tie the blindfold around his eyes. As the pair of young vampires watched in silence, he extended his arms and stuck out the index finger of both hands. Seba crouched low over the gushing water and held his position like a hovering hawk. For a long time he didn't move and his assistants were motionless too. Then, in a flash, his left hand shot into the water. When he pulled it out again, his finger was stuck through the middle of a small, silver fish.

Seba tossed the fish on to the bank, removed his blindfold and raised an eyebrow at Larten, inviting an apology. But Larten was in no mood to beg his master's forgiveness. With a curse, he suggested a dark, warm place where Seba could stuff the fish, then spun on his heels and stormed off.

"Larten!" Wester cried, struggling out of the stream. He wanted to go after his friend, but before he could, Seba called to him.

"Hold, Master Flack." When Wester looked back, he was astonished to see Seba smiling. "Let him go. It will do him good to sulk for a while."

Wester frowned, then looked for the fish. Picking it up, he sniffed carefully. "This isn't fresh," he whispered.

"I would be shocked if it was," Seba chuckled. "I caught it some hours ago, while you were hunting for my pheasant. I had it concealed up my sleeve. As a trained magician, Larten really should have noticed. Perhaps he was too hungry to concentrate."

"Larten was right," Wester snapped. "You're making fools of us."

Seba's smile faded and he shook his head. "You are like sons to me. I would never do that to you. The tasks I have set are all within the means of vampires of a certain standing. You and Larten are not yet ready to pass such tests, but they are legitimate and there is no shame in failing them."

"I don't understand," Wester frowned. "Why set the tests if you know we can't complete them?"

"To provoke a reaction like the one we have just seen." Seba sighed and stepped out of the water. "Larten is a fine young vampire, honest and obedient, but he lacks patience. He also tries to hide his true feelings. It is important for a man to control his emotions, but sometimes we need to be able to express ourselves freely in the company of those we love and trust.

"Larten needs to rebel," Seba said. "He has stood by me loyally ever since we met in that place of the dead, but the time has come for him to face the world by himself. He must choose his own path, not simply march with me down mine."

"Why don't you just tell him that and cut him free?" Wester asked.

"It is important that he thinks it is his own choice," Seba said. "If you have to be told to rebel, it is not a true rebellion." Seba noticed Wester's confusion and laughed. "You might have assistants of your own one night, and then my actions may not seem so curious.

"In the meantime I must ask you to trust me. Say nothing of this to Larten. Continue to suffer with him as he fails more tasks and grows ever angrier. If he asks how I reacted to his insults tonight, tell him I fumed and cursed his name. Let him think I am as angry with him as he is with me." Seba's eyes softened and his voice dropped. "By no means tell him that I love him dearly, or that this hurts me a lot more than it infuriates him."

CHAPTER TWENTY

The three vampires came to a city in the middle of the night. It was raining and they trudged through the streets in silence, keeping to the shadows. Larten and Wester were paying little attention to their surroundings, heads lowered, waiting for their master to find a spot where they could rest up. They assumed Seba would lead them to a graveyard or the ruins of an old building, as he usually did, but this time he surprised them by stopping in front of an inn.

"I feel like sleeping in a comfortable bed tonight," Seba said. "How does this establishment look to you?"

"Very nice," Wester said, beaming at the thought of spending the night indoors for a change.

"Fine," Larten grunted, casting a weary eye over the front of the inn. Then he paused and studied it again. It was an old-looking building, with blue glass in the windows. Not many inns had such curious glass.

In fact Larten had only ever seen one exactly like it, a long time ago, when he was still a human child and passed by this way quite often.

"I know this place," Larten whispered, raising his head and staring at the street with more interest.

"Do you?" Seba asked, faking innocence.

"I've been here before. This is..." He stopped and gulped. "This is the city where I was born."

Wester and Seba stared at Larten with surprise, though Seba's stare was forced. "Really?" Seba purred. "I had not thought. But yes, now that I cast my mind back, you are correct. It was in a graveyard not far from here where our paths first crossed, aye?"

Larten nodded slowly.

"Well, this is a nice surprise," Seba chuckled. "Or is it? Would you rather we move on and not spend the night here? It might stir up old memories. Perhaps we should—"

"I don't mind," Larten growled, feeling strangely uneasy, but not wanting to admit to his concerns. "It makes no difference to me. Stay or leave — I don't give a damn."

"Very well," Seba sniffed. "In that case we will stay. And, Larten?" He shook a finger from side to side when Larten looked at him. "*Do not.*"

*   *   *

The innkeeper was surprised to see three travellers abroad at such an hour, but Seba said they had been travelling in a carriage that had crashed when their horse lost its footing. The innkeeper expressed his sympathy, then gave them a reduced rate for the night – against Seba's protestations – and led them to their rooms, one for Seba and one for his assistants.

"A kind and generous gentleman," Seba noted as the innkeeper returned to his post. He turned questioningly to Larten. "Are all the people in your city of such fine standing?"

"Not that I recall," Larten said darkly, thinking about Traz and the way the foreman had murdered Vur Horston all those years ago.

"Well, perhaps they have improved in your absence," Seba smiled, then bid the pair goodnight and turned in.

Larten sat by the window in their room and said nothing, staring out at the darkness and the few people who passed by during the remainder of the night. He was remembering his old life, the days when he and Vur had set off to work each morning, fearing Traz's wrath, but pleased to be together, making wild plans for the future, dreaming of a time when they could break free of the factory and city and head off out into the brave, unexplored world beyond.

Wester kept a close watch on Larten. He was certain that this was no accident. Seba had brought them here on purpose. He guessed it was to get Larten thinking about the past, the path he had taken in life, the decisions he had made. Nothing could turn a person's thoughts towards the future more than a volley of ghosts from the past.

Wester didn't want to play Seba's game. He was worried where it would lead and what might happen to Larten if he rebelled as Seba wished. He was tempted to say nothing, keep his head down and hope that Larten stayed in the room until Seba announced that it was time for them to leave. But that would have been unfair. He could sense, by the way Larten shot him occasional glances, that his friend wanted to talk about this. So in the end he put his concerns aside and asked the question that Larten needed him to ask.

"Are you going to visit your family?"

Larten blinked as if the thought had never crossed his mind.

"What family would that be?" he replied.

"Your human family."

Larten shook his head. "I am no longer human. They mean nothing to me."

"They're still your family," Wester said.

"The members of the clan are my only family now,"

Larten insisted. "Vampires have no need of human relatives."

"But don't you want to find out what happened to them?" Wester asked. "Aren't you interested in their fate, if they're alive or dead, sick or well, successful or poor?"

Larten shrugged. "I put such concerns behind me when I became Seba's assistant. I serve him now. I do not wish to divide my loyalties."

"How can finding out what happened to your family result in a division?" Wester pressed. "It's natural to be concerned about those you were close to. Your family played a huge part in your life when you lived here. I know you were closer to your cousin than any of the others, but you still cared about them, and I'm sure they cared about you."

"I wouldn't be so certain of that," Larten huffed. "I bet they were glad to be rid of me — it meant more food for the rest of them."

"I doubt they were that cold," Wester said softly.

"You never met them, so how would you know?" Larten sneered.

"They were your kin," Wester said. "They shared your blood. They must have had some good qualities, or where did yours come from?"

"Don't try and flatter me," Larten growled, fighting to hide a warm smile.

"You know that I love you as a brother,"Wester said.

"Stop!" Larten winced. "You're going to make me cry!"

"Shut up,"Wester snapped. "I'm serious. I love and respect you, Larten, and have always looked up to you. But I'm envious of you too. Not because you're faster or stronger than me, or because Seba is much prouder of you than he is of me — don't deny it."

"I wasn't going to," Larten said.

Wester's face dropped. "Weren't you?"

Larten chuckled. "Well, *maybe* I was."

Wester grinned, then continued. "None of that matters to me. The reason I envy you is because you have family and I don't. I wouldn't trade my time as a vampire for anything in this world, with one exception. If I could restore life to my parents, brother and sister, I would. If it meant giving up my powers, turning my back on the clan, Seba and you, I wouldn't have to think twice. I miss them so much, even all these years later."

"But I wasn't as close to my family as you were to yours," Larten said quietly.

"All the same," Wester sniffed, "they *were* your family. If I had a chance to see Ma again, to listen to Da grumbling about the weather, to fight over some stupid argument with Jon…"

Wester fell silent. It was dawn outside. The two vampires sat in their room and watched the sun rising, the street outside coming into sharper focus.

After a while, Larten sighed and stood. "I'm going out."

Wester nodded, asked no questions, and said nothing for a few minutes. Then, when he was sure that Larten had left the inn, he raised his voice slightly and said, "He's gone."

In the room next to his came a muffled response from Seba. "Good."

Then the vampire master and his assistant lay back on their beds, separated by the thin wall, and stared anxiously at the ceiling, wondering where Larten would go and what he would find in the city of his long-lost youth.

CHAPTER
TWENTY-ONE

The city had changed vastly since Larten had fled from the factory. New factories had opened for business. Old houses had been torn down and rebuilt. There were whole streets and roads he didn't remember at all.

Yet much was as it had been, just a touch dirtier and dustier than before. The markets still existed, traders laying out their wares as they had when he was a child. Popular inns and taverns drew the same sort of rowdy customers. He passed familiar churches and government buildings.

The silk factory was gone. That surprised Larten. He had never considered the possibility that it might have shut down or moved premises. When he first came to the building, he thought he had made a mistake and turned around slowly a few times, searching for the factory. When he realised that he had come to the right spot, he studied the structure in front of him. Some windows and doors had been replaced, a couple bricked up and a few more added. The sign over the main door had been changed. Larten could not read the new name, but he could tell by the smell that the place had been converted into an abattoir. That seemed appropriate to Larten, given the bloodshed he had experienced on his final day here.

Larten thought of entering the building and asking about the silk factory and what had happened to it. But he decided it didn't matter. It made no difference to him whether the owners had gone out of business or moved on.

"I hope your ghost haunts this place," Larten muttered beneath his breath, staring at the building and thinking of Traz. "I hope you became a tortured soul when I killed you, damned to remain trapped here forever. It's all you deserve."

Larten spat on the pavement, then turned his back on the spot where the factory had stood and stormed away, pulling the collar of his coat up high, to shelter his neck as much as it could from the rays of the rising sun.

Larten moved faster now, aware that he didn't have much time. Even with his cap and coat, the light was starting to burn him. If he wanted to avoid a bad case of sunburn, he would have to conclude his business swiftly and get off the morning streets before the sun rose much higher. The midday world was no place for a creature of the night.

Larten hurried through the old neighbourhood, familiar to him even after such a long hiatus. This part of the city hadn't changed as much as other areas. The poor couldn't afford to tear down and rebuild as freely as the wealthy, so they had to make do with what they had. Some old buildings had crumbled and were nothing but ruins, and a few new hovels had been constructed, but for the most part the borough had not been touched by the passage of time.

When Larten came to the small, gloomy house that had once been his home, he felt his heart tighten and his eyes begin to water. Surprised by his reaction, he scowled and blinked away the tears. He almost turned and left without going any further, but he forced himself to skirt around to the yard at the back, so that he could not later accuse himself of fleeing from his painful memories.

The pair of barrels stood as they always had, full of water, one for drinking, the other for washing. Larten entered the yard and angled towards the latter barrel. He was not afraid of being challenged. It was late morning and anyone who lived here should be at work. If that wasn't the case and somebody was at home, he could simply claim to have stumbled into the wrong yard — all of the houses looked much the same from back here.

Larten didn't give much thought to the possibility that any of his family might still live here. It had been a long time. His parents had probably died, while his brothers and sisters would have almost certainly moved out to raise families of their own.

Larten stood over the barrel and stared down at his reflection. He remembered the last time he had done this, how he had immersed his head then studied the patterns formed by the orange dye from his hair swirling in the water. Vur had been alive then. They had set off laughing for the factory, no idea of what lay ahead of them. If he could go back and warn those two boys of what they could expect from the rest of that day, would they believe him? Or would they dismiss him as a crank, certain that nothing so awful could happen to a pair of harmless, innocent boys?

As Larten studied his melancholic expression, someone coughed inside the house and the back door began to open. Reacting instinctively, Larten leapt and grabbed hold of the wall to his left. He hauled himself up, then pounced on to the roof like a cat and spread himself flat. Edging forward, he studied the yard from a height, unseen and unnoticed.

An elderly man stumbled out of the house and shuffled to the barrel of drinking water. He dipped in a mug, filled it, then drank slowly, hand trembling, drops spilling from the mug and dripping from his lips back into the barrel. When he was finished, he paused and looked up at the sky to check the weather.

The man was Larten's father.

For a human of that time, Larten's father was ancient. He had outlived virtually all of the people he had grown up with, Larten's mother and several of his children too. His skin was wrinkled and stained with dark spots and patches. He was almost as skinny as a skeleton, and could not stand straight. His hair was long and untidily kept, caked with dirt. But despite its poor condition, it was a brilliant white colour. Traz's dye had kept its sheen even after all these decades.

Larten wanted to launch himself from the roof, throw his arms around the old man and announce his return. The pair could laugh and cry together, go for a drink in an inn, reminisce about the past and catch up on all that had happened since their paths were so cruelly parted.

But Larten was a vampire, a creature of immense speed and power, who had barely aged since he was blooded. How to explain his youthful appearance, his aversion to the sun, his need to drink blood? If his father had been younger and healthier, perhaps they could have reconnected. But Larten sensed that he would only throw the old man's world into disarray if he revealed himself now. His father was frail and elderly, surely not much longer for this life. It would be unfair to shock him. Better to let him live out his last few months or years in peace and quiet, troubled by nothing more than dark clouds in the sky and the threat of rain.

The old man muttered something beneath his breath, then dragged himself over to the wall that Larten had leapt on to. With much wheezing and coughing, he knelt and touched some dead flowers that had been set at the base of the wall.

"I'll get new flowers for you soon," Larten heard his father mumble. Then he picked out some of the decomposed petals and tossed them aside. He carefully rearranged the others as best he could, sighed deeply, closed his eyes and started to pray.

Larten didn't care to eavesdrop on such a personal, sensitive scene, but he could not rise and slip away without alerting his father to his presence. He didn't want to have to flee from his own flesh and blood, so he remained where he was, spreadeagled, trying to tune out the old man's words and afford him as much privacy as he could.

Larten was probably on the roof no more than fifteen or twenty minutes, but it seemed much longer, especially with the sun beating down on him. He breathed a sigh of relief when his father finally drew to a close, got to his feet and retreated back inside. Larten waited a few minutes to be sure the old man would not return, then lowered himself to the ground and stepped across to study the flowers.

There was an inscription on the wall, carved into the crumbling brickwork. Larten had never learnt to read, so he could not decode the sentences that his father had chipped out of the bricks. But there were two names at the bottom that he recognised instantly, having seen them written down many times in his youth.

Larten and *Vur*.

His father had been saying a prayer for the two boys who had been taken from him. All these years later, having experienced so much and seen so many people suffer and perish, his thoughts were still for the pair whom he had lost in such unfortunate circumstances.

Larten recalled his flight from the city after he'd killed Traz. He had not gone home, primarily because the mob would be looking for him there, but also because he had assumed that his parents would not miss him, that they would freely hand him over to those who wished to execute him.

If Larten had known how much his father loved him, and how great an impact his son's departure and Vur Horston's death would have on him, he would not have stayed away so long. He would have returned after a few years, to tell his father that he was alive and doing well. The pair could have kept in touch. Larten could have dropped in on the old man every so often, provided for him, given him money, medicine, anything he needed.

Guilt consumed Larten as he stood there in the yard, staring at his name and Vur's, remembering the past, thinking about how his father had laid flowers and said prayers for him. With a miserable, mournful moan, he staggered out of the yard, wiping tears from his eyes, fleeing as he had fled as a child, only this time not from a lynch mob, but from himself and the memories of who he had been and the people he had hurt.

Larten spent the rest of that day in the ruins of an old house, crammed into the remains of a larder, sheltered from the sun. He wept for a long time and begged forgiveness of the vampire gods, as well as the God his father had been praying to.

Eventually, as dusk was settling upon the city, Larten picked himself up, dried his cheeks and returned to the inn. Wester was relieved to see him again — he had started to fear that his friend might never come back.

"Are you all right?" Wester asked as Larten let himself in.

"No," Larten said, but he forced a weak smile. "You were right about family being important. I've been a fool. My apologies."

"You don't ever have to apologise to me," Wester said. He licked his lips and thought about asking what had happened to Larten. Then he decided he should not ask such a question. If Larten wished to talk about it, he would. If not... well, everyone was entitled to their secrets.

Shortly after Larten had cleaned himself up, the door to their room opened and Seba stood outside. "Are you ready to continue?" he boomed, acting as if he knew nothing of Larten's absence. "All well and rested?"

"Aye," Larten said softly.

"Good," Seba smiled. "I have quite a difficult task in mind for the pair of you tonight. It is time I started to seriously test you. The easy nights are behind us. You will have to really buckle down now."

Wester groaned and tried to share a rueful glance with Larten. But Larten did not react to their master's announcement. He was staring at the floor, thinking about the choices he had made, the sad old man with the flowers, wondering if he should have been so quick to pledge himself to Seba that night in the graveyard a lifetime ago.

CHAPTER TWENTY-TWO

Several weeks later, Seba and his weary assistants arrived at a town in the middle of a festival. It was late at night, but revellers still wove through the streets, singing and drinking. Seba had planned to push on, but Wester pleaded with him to stay — it had been a long time since they'd been able to enjoy a party such as this. In a rare bow to one of his assistants' wishes, Seba altered his plans and led them to an inn.

Wester went out to take part in the celebrations, but Larten stayed in their room. He was still morose, thinking about the past, his current position and if this was the life for him. These past weeks he had found himself questioning the route he had taken and feeling regret at what he had lost by becoming part of the clan. He knew he could never go back to the world of humans, but he didn't feel a true part of the vampire clan either. The doubts that he had experienced in Vampire Mountain returned and again he started to wonder if he might not be happier if he put the ways of the Generals behind him and sought a new challenge elsewhere.

Larten's dark spirits didn't lift in the morning. Unable to sleep, and tired of listening to Wester's snores, he rose not long after midday and went down to get some food. He found a seat close to a window but still in the shade, and watched people outside getting ready for another evening of delights. Children ran around freely, sticking up bunting and flowers wherever they could find a niche. Larten smiled ruefully as he thought of his own hard childhood. He wished there had been time for him to play like these children, but even before he went to work in the factory, his mother had kept him busy around the house and almost never let him out.

Looking at these humans, thinking again about his father, Larten brooded on all that he had sacrificed to become a vampire. He would never have a son or daughter to carry on his name and love him unreservedly. He couldn't sit out in the sun like the older men of the town and sip ale while watching the world roll by. His was a world of blood, darkness and battle. How much simpler life must be for these less powerful but far happier folk.

Larten stayed by the window for most of the day,

shifting to keep to the shade as the angle of the sun changed. He was in a thoughtful mood and he drank lots of ale. Vampires could tolerate more alcohol than humans, and he would have had to drink wildly to get drunk. But the ale did give him a warm feeling in his stomach, and despite his melancholy he found himself chuckling at his reflection in the glass every so often.

"Why so merry?" someone asked after his latest dry chuckle.

Larten blinked and turned. A pretty lady was standing by his table and smiling at him. She had long brown hair, warm eyes, and was dressed colourfully. Larten felt himself blush.

"I was... thinking about... something," he mumbled. He hadn't much experience of talking to pretty ladies.

"It must have been something nice," the woman pressed.

"Um. Yes. It was." Larten knew that he must sound like a simpleton and he felt his blush deepen.

The woman swung her hands slightly and tilted her head. She wanted Larten to ask her to sit, but he had no idea that she was interested in him. He thought she was a waitress. He downed his ale and held out the mug, grinning awkwardly.

The lady frowned. "I don't work here," she said.

"No?" Larten stared at the mug, not sure what to do with it. In the end he raised it to his lips again, as if there were a few drops still in it. He held the mug over his face until the lady shook her head, bemused, and turned away. Then he lowered it and breathed out heavily. He wasn't sure why, but he felt like he'd been running very fast.

Larten caught the lady's eye a few times after that — she was with some friends in a corner, working on garlands of flowers for the festival. He wanted to smile at her and invite her over, tell her he liked her hair, that the flowers were nice and he was sorry for acting so foolishly earlier. But every time he thought of speaking to her, his stomach clenched and his mouth went dry. In the end he stayed where he was, kept his head low and drank in silence, trying hard to convince himself that he enjoyed being alone.

Larten didn't want to go hunting when Seba and Wester came to fetch him at sunset. He hadn't said much to Seba since their argument in the stream. He'd tried to avoid the elderly vampire altogether, but that was hard when you were travelling in a small pack. Tonight he had a good excuse to give his master the cold shoulder.

Chapter Twenty-two

"I want to stay and enjoy the festival," he said. "You can hunt without me."

Seba's eyes narrowed and he thought about forcing Larten to accompany him. But then Wester said, "I'd like to stay too. Please, master. It will be fun. I had a good time last night, but the festivities were almost over when we arrived."

"Vampires should not mix with humans at times like this," Seba said. "We are hunters. We should hunt."

"Even hunters need a break now and then," Larten growled, gearing up for an argument.

Seba prepared a retort, but then he caught sight of somebody familiar walking past outside. He paused, put a name to the face and realised that this might be the stroke of luck that he had been waiting for. He shrugged. "Very well. I will hunt by myself. Enjoy your *night off*."

Larten and Wester stared at one another as Seba let himself out.

"That was too easy," Wester said suspiciously.

"He must be getting soft in his old age," Larten sniffed and ordered a mug of ale for Wester. They ate some food, then wandered out to explore the town.

The festival was hitting full swing as they strolled. People danced and sang. A pig roasted on a spit and young children watched it with hungry, impatient eyes, squealing with delight when drops of fat dripped into the flames and sizzled.

A street magician entertained a mesmerised crowd, but Larten wasn't impressed. He could have put on a much better show. He almost volunteered, but that would have drawn attention and it was better for vampires to keep a low profile.

Wester insisted they stop and watch a puppet show. He laughed with delight as two male puppets fought over an ugly stick woman who was actually a crocodile in disguise. She ended up eating both of the men. It was the sort of crude act that would have never been approved at the Cirque Du Freak, but Larten had to admit that the puppeteer was quite skilled and his lips twitched at a few of the jokes.

"That was great," Wester chortled as they moved on.

"It was passable," Larten murmured.

"The puppets looked like something Mr Tall might have carved."

"No," Larten said. "He creates realistic masterpieces. Those were just—"

An excited roar silenced him. They were passing an alley. He hadn't been paying attention, but when he heard the roar, he glanced up. A group of people was crowded around two men, cheering them on. Larten caught glimpses of fists flying. "A boxing match," he noted.

"Shall we go and observe?" Wester asked.

"Why not?" Larten grinned. "It is fun to watch humans beating each other up."

The pair moved into the alley and pressed through the throng. When they got to the front, they were confronted with a peculiar sight. Both boxers were large men, but one was massive, tall and broad, with hands that wouldn't have looked out of place on a giant. It should have been a one-sided contest, but the larger man wasn't defending himself. He just stood, letting his opponent punch him. And all the time he was laughing.

"Come on!" the bigger man shouted as his opponent panted and wiped blood from his hands. The blood hadn't come from the giant, but from the other man's knuckles, the skin of which had been torn up. "You can do better than that."

"I think he's tiring, Yebba," somebody else said. "Perhaps he would appreciate a rest."

"To hell with *rest*!" the boxer snarled and started hitting the larger man again, blow after blow to his chin and cheeks, without any noticeable effect.

Larten looked for the man who had spoken and found him sitting on a barrel, smoking a delicate pipe, surrounded by a handful of pretty, giggling women. The man was tall and thin, dressed in the finest clothes Larten had ever seen. His hair was carefully swept back and his face had been artfully painted. It was the person Seba had recognised earlier, and Larten remembered him too.

"You are Tanish Eul, are you not?" Larten said softly, slipping up behind the man on the barrel.

The vampire half-turned and glanced at Larten and Wester. His gaze flickered to their fingers and when he spotted the scars on the tips he relaxed. "You have the advantage of me, good sirs. I don't believe we've met…"

"You invited me to join you in a game of cards some years back," Larten said. "We were in a rather infamous mountain at the time."

Tanish squinted, then nodded. "Actually I *do* remember, which is a miracle given the amount of ale I drank at Council. You were in a foul mood and turned down my offer. You're Seba Nile's assistant, aren't you?"

"Aye. Larten Crepsley. And this is Wester Flack."

"Seba's other assistant," Wester clarified.

"A pleasure to meet you both." The cultured vampire held out his pipe to them. "Do you smoke?"

"No," Larten said.

"A shame. Perhaps I can introduce you to the pleasures of the pipe later. Are you here with your master on business?"

"We're with Seba," Larten scowled, "but not on business. He's off hunting. We decided to enjoy the festival."

"Men after my own heart,"Tanish cooed and slid off the barrel. "Ladies, I'd like to introduce you to some good friends of mine." The women around Tanish all curtsied and fluttered their eyelashes. Larten found himself blushing, as he had in the inn.

"Yebba!"Tanish yelled. "I'm bored. Let's move on."

The giant boxer groaned. "But it was just getting interesting."

"You can stay if you like,"Tanish sniffed. "I'm going."

Yebba scowled, then eyed up his opponent. He thought about hitting the human, but in the end just picked him up and held him over his head while the people around them jeered. "Do you surrender?" Yebba asked politely. The man cursed loudly. Yebba shook him hard, then asked again if he was ready to yield.

"Yes," the man moaned, his face having turned a pale green shade.

Yebba set down his defeated foe, then accepted a towel from one of the ladies and wiped sweat and blood from his face. "Where are we going?" he asked.

"Wherever there is fun, frivolity and lakes of ale," Tanish laughed and led the small group of vampires and their admiring ladies off into the night.

CHAPTER TWENTY-THREE

Larten's head was throbbing when he woke. He groaned, tried to get out of bed, but collapsed and lay on the floor in a huddle, shivering like a wet dog. "I'm dying," he whimpered.

"You're lucky," Wester croaked. "I think I'm already dead."

Larten looked up and spotted Wester sitting in a corner, holding a bucket, face as white as flour.

"Have we been poisoned?" Larten asked.

"Hangovers," Wester whispered.

"I thought vampires did not get hangovers," Larten said.

"You thought wrong," Wester replied, then thrust his head over the bucket.

"My fine, sensible, hard-drinking assistants!" Seba bellowed, opening the door and stepping into the room. He was grinning wickedly.

"Not so loud," Larten begged, jamming his hands over his ears.

"What was that?" Seba roared.

Larten scrunched his eyes shut and took deep breaths, trying hard not to be sick. "I'm never drinking again," he vowed.

"*I am*," Seba chuckled. "But beware of making promises you cannot keep. I am sure you will find your way back to the barrel once your head clears."

"Barrel?" Larten echoed.

"You each had a barrel of ale on your shoulder when you staggered home this morning," Seba said. "You were swigging from them, laughing about puny humans who could only drink from mugs. I put them out in the hall when I got up. I can fetch them for you if you would like some more."

"No!" Larten and Wester yelled.

"I need that bucket," Larten gasped.

"Get your own," Wester snapped.

Seba laughed again, then sat on Larten's bed and picked a flower from his groggy assistant's orange hair. "Where did this come from?" he asked.

Larten stared at the flower and shrugged.

"Have you been courting pretty maids?" Seba pressed.

"I can't remember," Larten said.

"I did not have you pegged for a romantic," Seba hummed, "but perhaps there is hope for you yet." He cocked an eyebrow at Wester. "Did you come home bearing flowers too, Master Flack?"

"I don't think so," Wester said, running a hand through his hair just in case.

"Perhaps it fell into your bucket," Seba said. "Have a look."

Wester almost got sick again at the thought of that.

"You are loving this," Larten snarled.

"Aye," Seba beamed. "You will too when you are my age. One of the few joys for old men is being able to relish the suffering of the young when they overindulge. Now, who would like a hearty breakfast? Bacon? Sausages? A leg of lamb? Runny eggs?"

Larten lurched to his feet, darted across the room and snatched the bucket from Wester just in time. When he sank back, wiping drool from his lips, Seba said, "While I would happily stay and watch you suffer for several more hours, time is against us. Get ready, gentlemen. We depart in five minutes."

"I'm not going anywhere," Larten groaned.

"I couldn't leave this room even if I wanted to," Wester agreed.

"Never mind your hangovers," Seba barked. "I gave you your freedom last night on the understanding that it would be a once-off. You have had your fun. Now it is time to resume training. We will hunt and then I will set a fresh test for you."

"To hell with your tests!" Larten shouted.

Seba's features darkened. "Do not take that tone with me," he growled. "I am your master and I demand respect."

"Then earn it!" Larten challenged him. "If you showed us some compassion and understanding, maybe we would return it."

"Compassion for a pair of self-pitying drunkards?" Seba snorted. "You acted like fools, so it is only fitting that you suffer. As for understanding... I understand all too well. You would rather stay here, recover from your hangovers, and go out carousing for *flowers* again, aye?"

"Aye!" Larten shouted. "Flowers and more ale, that's what we're after. Do you have a problem with that, old man?"

"No," Seba said calmly. "I will leave you to it. Good luck, gentlemen."

Seba started for the door.

"Wait!" Wester cried. "Where are you going?"

"To explore the night."

"But you're coming back, aren't you?"

Seba looked around at the crumpled sheets, the bedraggled vampires, the bucket of sick. "What is worth coming back for?"

"But... you can't mean... you're abandoning us?"

Seba stared at Wester, who looked distraught, then at Larten, who was trying unsuccessfully to look like he couldn't care less.

"I assume you crossed paths with Tanish Eul last night?" Seba said softly.

Wester blinked. "How did you know about Tanish?"

"Vampires usually bump into one another in towns like this. I was certain you would root out master Eul sooner or later, and that when you did, you would face a choice — come with me to continue your education, or stay and run wild with him. It seems that you have chosen the latter option."

"But it can't end like this," Wester protested, struggling to his feet. "We'll come with you. Give us a minute. We didn't mean what we said. Tanish isn't —"

"Peace, Wester," Seba said kindly. "This is not the end of your apprenticeship, merely a pause. You are aware of the Cubs, vampires who break from the clan for a few years or decades to enjoy life in the world of humans before committing themselves to the demands of the night. You and Larten need to spend some time with others of your age and attitude, to drink and chase women and do whatever it is that you long to do.

"When you have had your fun and wish to return to

the clan, I will be waiting, assuming the luck of the vampires is with me and I am still alive. We can resume where we left off."

"What if we do not want to return?" Larten asked quietly, not looking up at his master.

"That is your choice too," Seba said. "I make no demands of either of you." He stretched and smiled. "To be honest, I am glad to be rid of you for a while. I want to run by myself again. I have been a tutor for too long.

"I will keep in touch," he promised. "This is a small world and we will never be that far from one another. If you need me, I will come. If you wish to study by my side again, I will accept you back. And if you choose to leave the clan, I will wave you on your way and bear you no ill wishes.

"Even in death may you be triumphant."

With that Seba turned and let himself out, leaving a very sick and bewildered pair of young vampires to stare in silence at the door and wonder what on earth they were going to do next.

CHAPTER TWENTY-FOUR

Larten and Wester spent the next few hours recovering. Their heads slowly began to clear and by late evening they were even feeling peckish and slipped downstairs to chance some food. They ate hesitantly, wincing whenever somebody laughed or yelled.

"Wine for these good men!" someone shouted as they were finishing their meal. Tanish Eul slumped beside Wester and punched his arm. "How are your heads?"

"Awful," Wester groaned.

"I thought as much," Tanish chuckled, spearing a slice of meat from Larten's plate. "You drank like fish last night, which is fine as long as you're used to it."

"How come you're so cheerful?" Larten asked. "You drank even more than us."

"I've had lots of experience," Tanish said proudly. "In the end it all boils down to how dedicated you are.

If you spend decades training in Vampire Mountain, you become a keenly honed fighting machine. But if you spend those decades working on your drinking skills instead..." He winked.

The wine arrived and Tanish poured three generous measures. Larten and Wester stared at their glasses as if they were filled with sour milk.

"To your good health," Tanish toasted them and downed his wine with one gulp.

Wester and Larten shared an uncertain look, then Larten picked up his glass and drank half of it. He shivered, but forced a grin. Wester didn't want to look out of place, so he had a few sips and smiled shakily too.

"Excellent," Tanish said, pouring more for them. "We can't let these things get the better of us. It's like fighting a bear — if you suffer a beating, you have to bounce back and find an even bigger, tougher bear to pit yourself against. You drank a lot last night, but tonight we'll pump even more down your throats. We'll branch out a bit too. Have you ever sampled absinthe?"

"I don't know about that," Wester said sheepishly. "I don't think my head can take another lengthy session."

"Of course it can," Tanish hooted. "You'll feel worse than this tomorrow, believe it or not, but give it a few weeks and you'll start to find your feet."

"What makes you think we will be spending that long with you?" Larten asked.

"I saw Seba leaving town," Tanish said. "He didn't look like he was planning to return. He's left you to your own devices, hasn't he?"

Larten nodded glumly. "He told us we had to fend for ourselves, to join the Cubs and—"

"Wonderful news!" Tanish exclaimed. "He's handed you your freedom. So why are you looking miserable?"

"We don't know what we want to do," Wester sniffed.

"Our future was mapped out for us when we were training with Seba," Larten said. "We knew what to expect of the coming nights and years. Now..." He shifted uneasily. "Perhaps we could catch up with him if we set off immediately."

Tanish snorted. "Are you children or men? Do you want to be led around by your noses all your lives or stand up for yourselves?"

"That's easy for you to say," Larten snapped. "This is new to us. We did not plan it or know where to go from here."

"Go where the excitement is," Tanish said, then lowered his voice. "This is a thrilling, stimulating world for those willing to embrace it, especially those like us. We're stronger than humans, sharper, faster. We can drink and eat more than them. Beat them easily in contests. Earn the respect of any man, win the heart of any woman."

"But it's wrong to use our powers that way," Wester protested.

"Nonsense," Tanish said. "That's the way Generals think. You're Cubs now, free of the dictates of the clan. As long as we don't break the laws – by killing, for instance, or taking slaves – they leave us alone. Remember, many of the Generals have been in this position themselves. It's common for vampires to take a few decades to experience the pleasures of the human world. Think of these as your adolescent years."

"Maybe that's true," Larten said. "But we still do not know what to do next."

"That's simple," Tanish said and stood up. "Follow me."

He swept from the inn, and since Wester and Larten didn't have much choice, they stumbled after him. The fresh air revived them, but they weren't out in it for long. Tanish led them to a dark, smoke-filled tavern, where lots of women were pouring drinks for men and laughing at their jokes.

Tanish found a couch and made himself comfortable.

Larten and Wester sat stiffly beside him. Several eager women flocked to their side as soon as they were settled.

"Who are your friends?" one of the women crowed, perching herself on Larten's lap. He blushed a deep red and froze.

"Men of distinction and fine tastes," Tanish said loftily. "Bring us your best wine and finest dishes."

"I'm not hungry," Wester muttered, blushing too as a woman whispered in his ear. "I think I'll go back to—"

Wester started to rise, but Tanish pushed him down. "You'll stay and dine with me," he growled. "I'm your host tonight. If you refuse my hospitality, you'll insult me, and I don't forget an insult in a hurry." His eyes flashed dangerously and he held Wester's gaze.

Wester gulped, then said meekly, "As you wish, Tanish."

"Very good," Tanish purred. "That's what I like. I can see we're going to—"

Wester was on him before he could finish, the nails of his fingers pressed to the vulnerable flesh of Tanish's throat. Larten appeared on the vampire's other side, his nails aimed at Tanish's stomach.

"If you ever threaten me again," Wester snarled, "I'll finish this. Understand?"

Tanish smiled. "Congratulations. You passed."

"Passed what?" Wester snapped.

"The test I always set to determine whether or not I'll accept a man as a true friend." The women around them were staring at the trio uncertainly. Tanish crooked a finger at one of them, then pointed to a bowl of dates on the table. The woman passed him the bowl and he flipped a few dates into his mouth without attempting to push Larten or Wester away.

"My friends must be men of good character," Tanish said calmly. "I lead a wild, frenzied life, but I try to live honourably and I prefer to spend my nights in the company of honourable men. I will drink with the greatest of rogues, but when I travel, I only travel with men whom I respect.

"I insulted you in order to test you. For that, I apologise unreservedly. If you can forgive me, we will be the best of friends from this time on. If I went too far, I will bid you all of my best wishes as you take to the road without me."

Wester blinked and glanced at Larten. The orange-haired vampire shrugged to let Wester know that this was his call. Wester considered his options, then drew his nails away from Tanish's throat and sat again.

"How about that food?" Tanish asked as if nothing

untoward had happened. "Can I tempt you or are you truly too full to eat?"

"I could probably manage a few mouthfuls," Wester said.

"And wine?" Tanish asked Larten.

"Why not?" Larten smiled crookedly as someone poured a *very* large glass of wine for him.

At first Larten didn't say much. Tanish spoke at length about the pleasures the world had to offer, the great cities they would visit, the wars worth checking out. Women swept around them, offering dates, other food, wine, ale and more. A few tried to kiss Larten when they realised how shy he was, and ran away giggling when Tanish roared at them and pretended to lose his temper.

Wester was a bit braver than Larten, and was soon chatting to the ladies as if this was something he did all the time. He passed compliments, bought wine for them, even sang a couple of old vampire songs as the night progressed.

Tanish tried to involve Larten, but he kept shaking his head and hiding behind a mug of ale or glass of wine. Tanish eventually lost interest in the moody young vampire. When Larten was left alone on the couch — Wester had disappeared with a couple of girls who wanted to show him where the best wine in the tavern was stored — he felt like an outcast. Since he hadn't bought any drinks or entertained them in any way, the ladies were ignoring him. Nobody sat beside him or tried to talk to him.

Depressed and lonely, Larten drank more quickly than before, a mix of wine and ale. Remembering what Tanish had said, he ordered absinthe, but the barman had to show him the correct way to drink it, and even as a vampire he found it a bit too strong for his liking.

Larten decided he'd had enough. He got up and tried to leave, determined to go after Seba and beg his pardon. But he had drunk more than he realised, because his legs wobbled and he couldn't find his way to the door. As he staggered around, blinking dumbly, he spotted Tanish sitting at a table, playing cards with a group of serious-looking men. Larten's eyes swam back into focus and he grinned, seeing a way to be part of the good time that everybody else was having.

"Do you mind if I join you?" Larten asked, stepping up beside Tanish.

Tanish squinted at the woozy-looking vampire. "We're playing for high stakes," he warned. "This is no game for a beginner."

"That's all right," Larten smiled, taking a seat. "I have played before."

Chapter Twenty-four

"Do you have much money?" one of the other men asked.

"No," Larten said. "But I will have soon."

As the others laughed, he held out a hand for the pack of cards. Tanish passed them across, not sure whether or not he should let Larten play. As soon as the cards were in his hands, Larten started shuffling swiftly. As the other men stared, he shuffled at an almost impossible speed with his right hand, then passed the cards to his left hand and shuffled as equally fast with that one.

"You have hands like quicksilver," Tanish murmured, finding it hard to follow the movement of the cards, even though he was a vampire.

"Aye," Larten chuckled. "I know a few tricks too." Still shuffling one-handed, he let an ace slip from the pack on to the table without pausing, then another, the third and the fourth. He stopped and passed the pack to the man next to him. "But you have my word that I will not resort to trickery tonight. I will play fairly, and if I win, I will buy the most expensive drinks for everybody in the house."

The men cheered and a few of the ladies who were nearby came to sit close to Larten and admire his card skills. When he won his first hand, he passed a stack of coins to a beautifully dressed lady and told her to buy Champagne for all of them.

"Now there's a man with style!" Tanish exclaimed, slapping Larten's knee, delighted by this unexpected change in the previously solemn vampire. "You were slow to begin with, but I think you're getting the hang of fine living now, aren't you, my quick-handed friend?"

"Aye," Larten smiled, settling down for a long night of wine, women, gambling and whatever else came his way. "I think I might be cut out for this."

Across the room, in a particularly dark corner, a small man heard the boast and lifted his head. He was smartly dressed in an unusual yellow suit, and he had white hair, rosy cheeks and an amusingly styled pair of spectacles. From a distance he might have looked like a kindly grandfather, but up close nobody would have made such a mistake. There was something deeply unsettling about him, and although the tavern was busy, nobody drifted close to the short man's table.

"Cut out for fine living?" the man in the yellow suit purred. He cocked his head and his eyes went distant, as if he was looking at something a long way off. "Yes," he whispered. "And cut out for more too, if I'm any judge. I have been spying on Tanish Eul for some time now, but I think I will be keeping my eye on you instead from this point on, Master Crepsley. Is it coincidence that our paths crossed tonight?" He grinned twistedly and stroked a heart-shaped watch which was hanging from his breast pocket. "Or is it *destiny?*"

To be continued . . .

THE SAGA OF DARREN SHAN

❧ THE DEMONATA ❧